W9-BUF-395

TALENTS
· AND ·
TECHNICIANS

BOOKS BY JOHN W. ALDRIDGE

LITERARY CRITICISM

After the Lost Generation
In Search of Heresy
Time to Murder and Create
The Devil in the Fire
The American Novel and the Way We Live Now
Classics and Contemporaries: Selected Essays 1968–1991

FICTION

The Party at Cranton

SOCIAL COMMENTARY

In the Country of the Young

EDITED WORKS

Critiques and Essays on Modern Fiction
Discovery # 1
Selected Stories by P. G. Wodehouse

TALENTS

■ AND ■

TECHNICIANS

LITERARY CHIC AND THE NEW ASSEMBLY-LINE FICTION

■

JOHN W. ALDRIDGE

MIDDLEBURY COLLEGE LIBRARY

CHARLES SCRIBNER'S SONS NEW YORK
MAXWELL MACMILLAN CANADA TORONTO
MAXWELL MACMILLAN INTERNATIONAL
NEW YORK OXFORD SINGAPORE SYDNEY

Copyright © 1992 by John W. Aldridge

All rights reserved. No part of this book may be reproduced or transmitted in any form or by any means, electronic or mechanical, including photocopying, recording, or by any information storage and retrieval system, without permission in writing from the Publisher.

Charles Scribner's Sons
Macmillan Publishing Company
866 Third Avenue
New York, NY 10022

Maxwell Macmillan Canada, Inc.
1200 Eglinton Avenue East
Suite 200
Don Mills, Ontario M3C 3N1

Macmillan Publishing Company is part of the Maxwell Communication Group of Companies.

Library of Congress Cataloging-in-Publication Data
Aldridge, John W.
Talents and technicians: literary chic and the new assembly-line fiction / John W. Aldridge.
p. cm.
Includes index.
ISBN 0-684-18789-2
1. American fiction—20th century—History and criticism. 2. Fiction—Technique. I. Title.
PS379.A5198 1991
813'.5409—dc20 91-35894 CIP

Macmillan Books are available at special discounts for bulk purchases for sales promotions, premiums, fund-raising, or educational use. For details, contact:

Special Sales Director
Macmillan Publishing Company
866 Third Avenue
New York, NY 10022

Design by Janet Tingey

10 9 8 7 6 5 4 3 2 1

Printed in the United States of America

For Patsy

Whoever comes to the gates of literature without the Muses' madness, believing that technique alone will make him an adequate writer, is himself ineffectual, and the writing of this sane man vanishes before that of the man who is mad.

PLATO, *Phaedrus*

Compared with the short stories of our day, those of Turgenev look like Delacroix's battle scenes reduced to the size of medallions. There is constant tragedy. In our own stories the horizon of birth and death has been removed to such a distance in time and space that people live in a state of lukewarm immortality, briefly upset now and then by episodes of loss or even terror and ruffled otherwise by the half-hearted oscillations of daily experience.

RUDOLF ARNHEIM, *Parables of Sun Light*

▪

▪ ACKNOWLEDGMENTS ▪

The opening chapter of this book was first published in *The American Scholar* (Winter 1990), and the discussion of Don DeLillo's *White Noise* formed part of a review that appeared in the *Chicago Tribune Book World* (January 13, 1985). I wish to thank the editors for their permission to reprint. All the other materials are published here for the first time.

I owe special thanks to Katharine McGovern and Daniel J. Lyons for sharing with me their views of some of the writers discussed here and stimulating my interest in the further discussion this book represents. McGovern was particularly helpful by offering her own younger perspective on her near contemporary, Lorrie Moore, and indicating the areas of Moore's work that have special significance for her generation. I have learned from both of these extremely perceptive young readers.

▪ CONTENTS ▪

▪ PREFACE ▪

The idea for this book was in part suggested to me by Norman Mailer, although he was not aware of it at the time and is surely in no way responsible for the result. But in an introduction he wrote in 1985 to a new edition of my first critical book, *After the Lost Generation*, he very generously credited the book with providing the fiction writers of his and my age with their first distinct sense of themselves as a literary generation. He then went on to speculate as to whether or not the current group of younger writers will be similarly treated by a critic functioning as I functioned then.

That speculation was one of the factors that led me to decide, for better or worse, to undertake the job myself. But what I ended by producing is clearly not the book Mailer presumably had in mind, nor, for that matter, is *After the Lost Generation* quite the book he seems to have recalled through the blessedly sanitizing mists of memory. My treatment of the post–World War II literary generation was considerably more negative than he appears to believe, although of the writers I discussed, he himself and three or four others came off quite well.

However, my position then and in the books I have since published was and has remained essentially adversarial, partly, I suppose, for reasons of innate perversity but also because I believe that that is a necessary position for a critic to take. Particularly in the early years of my career, when I was afire with rectitude, I took it as gospel that the first responsibility of the critic is to function as a monitor of taste, to challenge fashionable opinion, whether it is the opinion of the popular audience or of the literary establishment, simply on the ground that it is fashionable and therefore suspect. I also saw it as an essential if somewhat dangerous critical duty to perform a deflationary operation on certain writers when it seemed that their reputations had become unjustifiably enlarged.

Of the writers whose fiction I have selected for discussion here, all but one—the late Raymond Carver—are relatively young and have become well known, even in a few instances famous, quite early in their careers and over a period of only a dozen or so years. Their books have been widely and, for the most part, enthusiastically reviewed and have attracted a substantial readership, albeit mostly among people of roughly their own age. Fashionable opinion appears to have decreed that they are the most promising and attractive talents among the hundreds of young writers now at work in this country, and that they may even be considered to be in their various ways the chief representatives of the literary concerns and attainments of their generation.

But a curious fact about these writers, and one I discuss in some detail in the book, is that such reputations as they have acquired are mainly the products of book reviews, literary gossip, and publishers' advertising and have scarcely come under examination or been ratified by serious criticism. This has prompted me to attempt such an examination here, although it will become evident that I have only occasionally been moved to ratify.

This, then, is a study deliberately limited to the work of a selected few of the current younger writers who have received the largest amount of attention and praise. In it I have tried to determine what virtues of their fiction account for their public prominence, and to what extent that prominence seems justified; what are their artistic preoccupations, strengths, and limitations; and what do they have to say of importance about contemporary American experience. I have had no intention of producing the kind of book that attempts to survey every trend, tremor, and talent on the literary scene, nor have I discussed every short story and novel these writers have produced. Instead, I have limited myself to those works that seem to represent most clearly the nature and quality of their literary achievement as a whole. If I have frequently questioned the size of that achievement, I have done so not only because I believe that some of these writers have been overrated but because the question has not been raised often enough, and that is clearly a bad thing for them and a worse thing for literature.

John W. Aldridge
Ann Arbor, Michigan
September 1991

CHAPTER 1

THE NEW ASSEMBLY-LINE FICTION

In two special issues appearing twenty-four years apart, in 1963 and 1987, *Esquire* magazine published feature articles purporting to indicate just where the major centers of literary power are located in the United States and which writers have the greatest influence on the course of national literary affairs. When studied side by side, the two sets of findings provide the basis for some illuminating insights into the nature of the American literary life as it has evolved or, depending on one's point of view, devolved over the last quarter-century.

Much of the information given in the two issues is presented through the medium of double-page maps on which persons and places considered by *Esquire* to be literarily important are located. On the 1963 map these are designated in a fairly prosaic fashion, with specific areas of artistic interest marked out in different colors according to their roughly terrestrial placement under headings like "Squaresville," "Ivory Tower," "College Campuses," and "The Cool World."

But the format chosen for the 1987 presentation clearly embodies an attempt at something far more grandiose. Any resemblance to the Earth is erased from the map, and what is depicted is spectacularly cosmological. The persons and places possessing the greatest concentration of literary power are represented now as Stars, Novae, Ursae Majores, and Media Showers, and by the various signs of the Zodiac. In short, by 1987 the map has become a perfect mirror for the present age of show business celebrity and glitz. In slightly more than twenty years it seems we have arrived at such a hyped-up condition of euphoria that we no longer see ourselves as dealing with mere places and people but as inhabiting a literary cosmos sparkling with the first-magnitude incandescence of Heavenly Bodies.

The implications of this change may be easily inferred from the differing contents of the two maps. Dominating both is a flaming red area—in 1963, a large and untidy smear of color extending over a good quarter of the map; in 1987, a small, neat circle about the size of a doughnut—representing that privileged locale known as "The Red-Hot Center." Placed here are the names of personages deemed by *Esquire* to possess the highest status in the literary community. Interestingly enough, in the "Center" of 1963 appear literally dozens of names of serious writers and critics, some of whom are grouped together according to publishers or the various agents representing them. The long list of "Working Critics," about a third of whom occupy the "Center," is itself extremely impressive and includes, among many others, such authorities as Edmund Wilson, Malcolm Cowley, Alfred Kazin, and Dwight Macdonald. Also falling within the "Center" in 1963 are the names of writers listed under the titles of two prominent literary magazines—*Partisan Review* and *The Paris Review*—to which at the time they were contributors. Writers for *Commentary*, *The Hudson Review*, *Story*, and *Contact* are listed but in a yellow area outside the "Center," along with a number of others associated with the more prestigious creative writing programs at

Iowa, Stanford, Columbia, and elsewhere. The major publishers and agents are included with their better-known clientele, and in addition to the list of "Working Critics," there are even separate categories in the area designated as "Ivory Tower" for "Academic Critics" (Lionel Trilling, Hugh Kenner, et al.) and "Theoreticians" (René Wellek, Northrop Frye, et al.).

The 1987 map is an altogether different affair. To be sure, there are comparable and extensive listings of writers under the rubric of their publishers and agents. In fact, this kind of material occupies a far larger area this time than it did in 1963, the implication being that the business affiliations writers have with publishers and agents have assumed much greater importance than they were seen to have twenty-four years before, while other formerly important adjuncts of the creative process—literary magazines and critics—have become quite irrelevant. And this impression is confirmed by the complete disappearance from the 1987 map of all listings of academic and theoretical critics and magazines, even though both continue to exist and may even be said to have increased in number over the last twenty-five years. Also missing are the names of poets and the kinds of writers who were designated in 1963 as belonging to the avant-garde and who were included under the heading of "The Cool World," their absence in 1987 presumably implying that poetry and experimental writing no longer exist or, at any rate, no longer count because, after all, they don't sell.

Interestingly enough, the only critics named on the 1987 map are daily or weekly reviewers for large-circulation publications like *The New York Times, Publishers Weekly, Time, Newsweek*, and *The Washington Post*. This would seem, on the face of it, rather baffling because it represents a complete reversal of opinion. In 1963, such reviewers were contemptuously banished to a Siberian exile colony designated on the map as "Squaresville." But now they have been restored not only to major prominence but, given the absence from the map of the other kinds of critics, to sole critical authority, quite as if their responses to books are the only responses that matter these days.

But perhaps most astonishing of all is the placement of a daily *New York Times* reviewer, Michiko Kakutani, within the 1987 "Red-Hot Center" as the only critical commentator who, according to *Esquire*, is taken at all seriously by serious people. The remarkable feature of this elevation to high office is that in her relatively short tenure at the daily *Times* Kakutani has shown herself to be an assiduous consumer of new books, mostly of fiction, without displaying more than minimal ability to distinguish one from the other. The fact that the book under review was written by a new or a recently-become-trendy author is enough to earn it Kakutani's unqualified praise. And since she is almost uniformly consistent in this reaction, she has become a powerful publicist who could not do a better job if she were in the employ of the American Booksellers Association. Therefore, given the current ascendancy of hype over critical discussion, it is undoubtedly only fitting that her name should appear in the "Red-Hot Center."

But the presence there of some of the other names is more problematical. Of the hundred or so appearing in the space in 1963, just two—Mailer and Bellow—reappear in 1987, and they are joined by only nine others. In addition to Kakutani, the newly elected are Raymond Carver; Gary Fisketjon, who, in *Esquire*'s words, is "the only young editor . . . who has the power—and the inclination—to publish his contemporaries"; Robert Gottlieb, the Knopf editor recently appointed to the editorship of *The New Yorker*; Elmore Leonard, a best-selling writer of blockbuster thrillers; Gordon Lish, "an author, editor, teacher, and publisher" and prolific encourager of young literary talent; Gayfryd Steinberg, a rich and beautiful giver of parties and, until recently, chief patroness of PEN; John Updike; and, finally, Amanda ("Binky") Urban, a literary agent whom *Esquire* considers the hottest around.

What is significant about this list is that it includes not one important critic, just three writers of established reputation, one writer (Carver) of some talent but minor stature, a commercial hack, and five people, their names comprising nearly half the list, who are publishers, editors, agents, or, in the case of Steinberg, philanthropic supporters of the arts. As *Esquire* itself admits, "Today, in place of the hipster, we have the hypester," and it is obvious that indeed we do. But to put the matter more bluntly, one might say that in place of serious, independent writers—only the most celebrated of whom are represented on the list—we have merchants operating a vast corporate enterprise engaged in the mass manufacture and promotion of books; merchants, furthermore, who wish to be as free as possible from, and would like to deny the existence of, the quality controls that serious criticism might impose on their products.

That is perhaps one important reason why the centers of critical activity and influence that were depicted on the 1963 map as scattered abundantly across the country, mostly at universities, are almost entirely omitted from the map of 1987. In their place the regions where writers live and party together (the Hamptons, Connecticut, Martha's Vineyard) are given prominent position, as are the names of the people who are best known for giving the parties (George Plimpton, Jean Stein, and again Gayfryd Steinberg). Obviously, the only center that counts now is located in New York and its immediate environs. Everything that can be considered remotely important in literary style and endeavor is produced or is huckstered, sold, and consumed there.

And the additions to and deletions from the 1987 map make it very clear exactly what has happened to create this monolithic and self-protective concentration of power. Although the symbiotic relationship between serious criticism and the production of literature, while regrettably thin in the best of times, has clearly deteriorated badly over the last twenty-five years, the 1987 map, by showing it to have disappeared altogether, generates the most useful illusion—at least for the publishing business—that the only criticism worthy of notice is the work of daily and weekly reviewers.

These are the people whose function it is to report regularly on newly published books, but who, because of limitations of time and space, are nearly always forced to treat them superficially and, for the most part, favorably—that is, with emphasis on those qualities that will be attractive to the avid company of book buyers, so many of whom evidently choose to buy books because they are recommended by reviewers but read them the way they consume made-for-television films and would be hard-pressed the next day to remember what they had read or watched the night before.

Such a situation makes it possible for literary products to be touted and sold on the market without having to pass more than minimal critical inspection and in some instances to become briefly appealing for altogether meretricious reasons. The novels of Jay McInerney and Bret Easton Ellis, for example, are by any serious critical measure artistically empty works that are best-sellers largely because they depict a spiritually empty world that is attractive to readers who are themselves spiritually empty and so in reading them experience a faint twinge of self-recognition. But considering the popularity of these works, there is no reason for publishers or reviewers to give public notice to such a subversive consideration. And if the critical community does not give it public notice or is not heeded when it does, then there exists no means by which the reading audience can be influenced in the making of critical judgments.

All this would seem to put these writers and some of their contemporaries in an extremely bizarre position, for they have come to public attention and been installed in a kind of modest eminence without first having had to earn that eminence through the accretion around them of responsible critical opinion deeming them worthy of it. On the strength of some favorable or not unfavorable reviews and through being named in survey articles as forming with one another an important new literary group, they have become familiar names known mostly for being familiar names.

At the very least they are likely to be left floundering in a dilemma similar to the one I half-facetiously described in *Time to Murder and Create* (1966) right after the first *Esquire* survey appeared in 1963 as overtaking hypothetical young writers whose names had been favored for inclusion in the "Red-Hot Center."

> It is not so very surprising that there should be young one-or-two-book writers today who seem to feel no particular obligation to settle down to their proper business of writing more books, since they already enjoy most of the advantages of having written them without having had to. It is not surprising *if* one remembers . . . that what we are dealing with here is actually not a literary world at all, but a publicity and celebrity world, in which the writer simply as personality or public phenomenon can achieve, if he is lucky, a status comparable in kind, if not in scope, to that of movie stars and political figures, but in which his status may have little or nothing to do with his contribution to literature.
>
> The fact that it is not genuine literary status he enjoys

may or may not trouble his conscience. It very probably will not, for the counterfeit that he does enjoy is what passes for the real thing in the world in which he so successfully makes his way, and it would be absurd to expect him to take quixotic risks for the sake of a principle that would be certain not to pay off. The respect of his peers and contemporaries, the support of an informed and genuinely interested readership, the benefits to be derived from a criticism that senses and attempts to define the real values in his work—all these may be nice idealisms to which now and then his mind dreamily recurs. But he is far too ambitious and practical to be willing to wait for the revolution that might one day turn them into realities. Besides, if they ever became realities, who knows what might happen to his career?

The principal difference between the situation in 1963 and the situation today is that the problems created for young writers by publicity overkill have if anything worsened. Where in 1963 I could charge that serious criticism was at fault for treating the work of such writers as literary phenomena, as *objects* of analysis and textual commentary, quite apart from any really close engagement of their quality as artists, it is now possible for *Esquire* in its vaudevillian conception of the literary marketplace to leave criticism out of account altogether and to give over the entire evaluative function to book reviewers.

Yet to be fair one has to admit that this has not occurred just because the moguls of the marketplace have chosen for self-protective reasons to deny the existence of criticism. Nor in this cynical age can they be blamed for seizing the quite uncontested opportunity to generate a climate in which publicity rather than solid achievement produces reputation.

Publishers, after all, may dream of becoming benevolent middlemen for the creation of deathless masterworks, but they are in the highly mortal business of manufacturing commodities that sell.

The fact is that the major responsibility for the failure of serious criticism to exert a corrective influence in the marketplace—and its consequent disappearance from the 1987 *Esquire* map—must be borne by criticism itself as well as by the periodicals that once provided it with an outlet and an audience extending beyond the walls of academia. Until fairly recently it was possible for the people *Esquire* listed as "Working Critics" to publish essay-reviews—often as long as 3,000 to 4,000 words—that discussed at some depth current books of consequence or inconsequence and that were addressed to a general well-educated readership. Periodicals like the New York *Herald Tribune Book Week, The New Republic, The Nation, Saturday Review*, even now and then *The New York Times Book Review*, once gave considerable space to such commentaries and often allowed critics to appear on a fairly regular basis so that they had access to a continuing medium for the development of their ideas. Before the book section was abolished altogether in the early 1980s, it was even possible to find long and closely evaluative critical essays in *Harper's*, and throughout the 1970s *Saturday Review* published such material on a regular basis.

But these outlets have dramatically declined in number. The New York *Herald Tribune Book Week* suspended publication many years ago. *Saturday Review* had ceased by 1980 to print reviews longer than snippets of a hundred words or so, and *The New Republic* and *The Nation* are providing less and less space for discussion of imaginative literature.

Over the past two decades there has been a massive acceleration in the pace of the movement that first became visible in the 1950s and has brought increasing numbers of literary people to the universities, many of whom might in a more hospitable time have become independent working critics. In academia today, at least among younger faculty, the criticism of contemporary literature flourishes to the point where it has achieved the proportions of a major industry. Yet very little, if any, of it affects the production or reception of this literature in the marketplace. For one thing, it is mostly theoretical and analytical rather than evaluative in approach, and for another, it is nearly always published in journals that are virtually unknown to the general reading public.

But the factor that is perhaps most responsible for preventing academic criticism from having a vital influence on the public reception of new work is that it is concerned almost exclusively with work that is not only no longer new but is the product of contemporary writers whose reputations are solidly established and whose suitability as objects of study cannot, therefore, be seriously questioned. Where in an earlier time working critics, writing for *Saturday Review* or *The New Republic*, might discover and take the risk of promoting new literary talents, the academic critics concern themselves primarily with investigating the ambiguities to be found in, or testing various deconstructionist theories on, the work of already canonized talents like Bellow, Mailer, Heller, Vonnegut, and Updike. And they most emphatically do not do this in the course of reassessing those talents or to raise subversive doubts as to whether they deserve the high prestige that they currently enjoy. Academic critics tend by nature and calling to be reluctant to give their attention to any work that is not already thoroughly ground in the mill of the orthodox.

There are, to be sure, certain other writers such as

Pynchon, Barth, DeLillo, Coover, Gaddis, and the brothers Barthelme who form what at one time would have been called an avant-garde of American fiction writers, whose work is difficult enough to invite scholarly explication, and who, partly because of that difficulty, have not achieved really large reputations among the general reading public. Yet even in relation to this technically radical, albeit not exactly new group, there is very little disagreement among academic critics over the question of their relative merits. In fact, that question is very seldom raised, almost as if through some silent critical consensus it had been declared irrelevant. For somehow these writers have already been selected to become prime candidates for assimilation into the official establishment of contemporary writers, their principal thematic and formal characteristics having by now been extensively documented, graphed, cross-referenced, disinfected of mystery, and made safe for classroom consumption. And if the general public in its ignorance has not yet come to recognize just how important these writers are, then that, in the academic view, is simply further proof that they are important.

Yet it must be said that academic criticism at its best is the most sensitive and informed criticism now being written about contemporary literature, and its failure or its refusal to communicate with the literary marketplace and the general reader cannot help but have a damaging effect upon newer writers such as those so vigorously touted by *Esquire*. It has left them, as I have said, quite obviously in a kind of standardless void and at the mercy of the book reviewers and the various agencies dedicated to the promotion of their books. Their situation, in fact, is an exceedingly strange one, and their presence on the literary scene has about it a peculiar ghostly quality.

Where in 1950, for example, there may have been ten or fifteen new young writers of some evident promise competing for critical and public attention, there now appear to be hundreds, mass-produced as if by machine. And it is often extremely difficult to distinguish one from the other, not only because so few of them engage the attention in an interesting and provocative way, but because so many of them seem to be interchangeable in their manner of writing, as if the machine that produced them specialized in turning out carbon copies. Their first books may be reviewed politely, even respectfully, because they are nothing if not well-schooled journeymen in the craft of composition. But following the appearance of those books they seem to drop into a swamp of oblivion without leaving a ripple on the surface and are not heard of again until their next books appear. Nothing in the interval seems to accrue around their names or their work, no curiosity about their personalities, no animated discussion of their writing, no critical debates over their artistic merits and demerits.

One must, however, concede the point that most of these writers seem to be more notable at least at the moment for what they are not than for what they are, and it may be that their current dilemma is at least partly a consequence of that fact. In sharp contrast to the young Hemingway, Fitzgerald, Mailer, Heller, Salinger, and Vonnegut, they have not attracted attention because of the distinctiveness of their writing styles or the originality of their use of the standard fictional forms. Their books have not so far created new circuits in the public imagination or provided the charged symbols for a new vision of the human condition in our time, nor has their language enlarged the vocabulary with which we describe the most urgent problems and preoccupations that concern us.

There appear to be among them no exotic personages on the order of the precocious, androgynous-looking young Capote, Vidal, and McCullers, no equivalents of the young

Mailer and Jones who together produced the first important novels to come out of World War II, no replacements for Heller and Vonnegut who provided the terms for a fresh comic vision of the institutionalized absurdities of American life. These writers and a certain few of their contemporaries generated some real excitement, at least during the years when they were producing their early—and in the case of some of them, their finest—work. But their descendants today—even those like Raymond Carver and Ann Beattie, who are perhaps the best known—appear destined to join the host of people who will enjoy the experience of being famous for fifteen minutes. All of them seem poised perpetually at the starting gate of genuine literary reputation, waiting to run a race that somehow cannot be concluded in favor of any winner because no one can define the terms by which a winner will be chosen.

■ II ■

The newer writers now beginning to become known for their first work or, in a few fortunate cases, already famous enough to be represented on the *Esquire* map belong to the first literary generation in American history—or, for that matter, in any history—ever to be created almost exclusively through formal academic instruction in creative writing. Unlike some of the most prominent members of the older generation—Pynchon, Mailer, Heller, and Vonnegut, among others—who have neither been formally trained to write nor become full-time teachers of writing, a surprising number of their descendants are the products of the advanced-degree writing programs that began proliferating around the country in the 1960s and that have since had more to do than any other force with shaping the characters of the writers they instruct as well as the literature those writers produce.

In fact, the various differences between the typical neophyte writers who are graduates of these programs and their predecessors in all previous generations are dramatic and extremely instructive because they illustrate the remarkable changes that have occurred in the ontogeny of literary apprenticeship in very recent times.

The most significant of these changes is also the most obvious. The process by which a young person traditionally awoke to the discovery that he had somehow become a writer was until now almost always a mysterious, painful, and lonely one. There had occurred at some unknown time in the turbulence of his psychic life an accidental conjunction of experience and temperament that brought the discovery about, most often in a state of relative social isolation and most assuredly not as a result of benevolent collective or institutional effort. American writers, in particular, perhaps because they are not naturally nurtured here, have, at least in modern times, usually been, like Auden's Yeats, hurt, irritated, or provoked into becoming writers by their sense of estrangement from a culture that has been provincially inhospitable, if not downright hostile, to the kind of human beings they found themselves to be or that subscribed to a system of values that they saw either as irrelevant to their deepest concerns or as utterly monstrous.

Very often in childhood they were driven to literature as an unconsciously sought alternative to more damaging emotional disturbance, as a means of escaping their feelings of social isolation, and at the same time of finding in the fictive world of books a confirmation of values more civilized and humane than those in force in the world around them. And eventually they learned to write from reading literature, not from taking courses, by slow degrees forming their literary standards on the work of the best writers and in defiance of the standards of those they ultimately recognized to be the worst.

In view of all this, it is not surprising that over the last hundred or so years American writers have in the main been highly individualistic in their manner in writing and adversarial in their attitudes toward the established culture. As a rule, they have been self-taught and self-motivated, working alone or in only brief proximity to one another and finding little imaginative sustenance in American life except material for books that so often and so poignantly revealed just how little sustenance they had found in American life. Perhaps this is a way of saying that they have been blessed or cursed with that sense of otherness Henry James spoke of as the primary psychic orientation of the natural writer or at least the natural American writer. For their characteristic stance has been that of the alien visitor from outer space or the lone civilized human being set down among savages. Their cultural estrangement, regardless of the many ingratiating guises and disguises it may have assumed, has, in the case of some of them, been such that it has endowed their best work with a kind of subversive clarity of vision in which experience is rendered often through a concentration on realistic detail so obsessive that it seems at times to border on the paranoid.

This development is one of the major reasons why iconoclastic realism became established as the dominant mode of American fiction, and it remained dominant for most of this century, leading to the production of some of the most vital and acerbic novels ever to appear in our literary history. In their profound disaffection with American life many of our writers have given us our most brilliantly realistic portraits of that life. Yet there has also been visible in our fiction a contrary strain that in recent decades has grown much more visible, the tendency of certain of our writers to express their disaffection in ways that push beyond the limits imposed by conventional realism into areas in which realistic details may become transformed into metaphors that embody more fully and precisely than realism the particular character of the writer's disaffection.

An early example of this is John Dos Passos's *USA,* a fictional trilogy usually considered, at least in its central narrative, to be a work of classic realism. Yet it soon becomes obvious that *USA* is not a portrait of any realistically observed America but of a country hallucinated by a malevolent economic conspiracy that has reduced the inhabitants to the condition of slavish automatons in whom all human qualities have been compromised or corrupted. Realism has, in this case, capitulated to political ideology. But behind ideology lies the paranoia of John Dos Passos directing him in the metaphorical portrayal of a culture that is the destroyer of values he believes to be transcendental.

Still earlier and very different examples of this same tendency can be found as far back as the novels of Hawthorne and Melville, which are not, at least in our modern sense of the term, realistic works nor are they works of cultural or political disaffection. Yet some of them give the impression that they are taking place in a sanctified vacuum virtually uncontaminated by the presence of people because the imaginative eye of their authors is so firmly fixed on the cosmos and the heavenly warfare of good with evil. In their case, the disaffection might appear to be with the whole secular world that is there in the novels, one might say, on sufferance and to stand as metaphor of the debasement of the sacred.

Interestingly enough, there are indications that this form of cosmic or mystical vision has resurfaced in a good many of our novelists at the present time. One finds evidence of it in the highly convoluted "systems" novels of Don DeLillo and William Gaddis in which the primary interest lies not in a realistic depiction of the social scene but in the intricate choreography of fictional motifs, the interplay of thematic forces within the narrative ecology, which become in effect an esthetic replacement for, and a considerable improvement upon, the social scene. This vision is present in a much more obvious way in such a work as Mailer's *An American Dream*, where the cityscape of New York is used as a phantasmagoric secular backdrop for the Manichean battle being waged between God and Satan for the moral courage of the protagonist, Stephen Rojack. It is there also in the dark fables of Kurt Vonnegut, which caricature the ills and deceits of our society and so in some degree palliate his and our fears that they will lead us to Armageddon.

These and similar novels are burdened by a heavy weight of abstract speculation—often generated by a realism of detail that one sometimes feels is present simply to serve as its launching platform—about the meaning of sin, guilt, redemption, bureaucratic totalitarianism, political corruption, the tyranny and treachery of sex, the psychopathology of violence and murder—all perhaps in some degree compensations for the failure of the writers to find sufficiently meaningful experience in the quotidian life of the culture and so needing to seek out and confront the extremes of moral and esthetic possibility in some transcendental sphere above and beyond the quotidian.

Alexis de Tocqueville observed with great prescience that in a democracy such as ours "each citizen is habitually engaged in the contemplation of a very puny object: namely, himself. If he ever looks higher, he perceives the immense form of society at large or the still more imposing aspect of mankind. . . . What lies between is a void." As so many of our contemporary novels amply demonstrate, American writers have continued to devote much of their energies to the contemplation of their puny selves. But when not so occupied and they have looked higher, they have tended to fill the void between with portraits of society at large and mankind in general, portraits that often swell to the dimensions of allegory, myth, and the more technical abstractions of metafiction and fabulation.

By contrast, the British, whose literature has traditionally been the kind Tocqueville described as typical of aristocratic societies, have gone on producing work that is generally far less ambitious in scope than ours, more firmly rooted in the social actualities, and much more agreeable and affectionate in its rendition of those actualities. It is, for the most part, a literature that is stoutly secular and pragmatic in its interests and that seems to possess little tolerance for abstract moral speculation. Perhaps because British writers appear not to suffer from our form of cultural estrangement, they can observe their society with a greater equanimity and dispassion and with a livelier because untraumatized fascination with its foibles and idiosyncrasies. Even when they are satirical, as they so often are, their attitude seems to be one of genial delight over the observed pretensions rather than the usual American attitude of horror and disgust.

It would seem that at least in this regard the younger generation of university-trained American writers resemble the British more closely than they do their literary predecessors in this country, for they too seem not to be estranged from their culture, if only for the reason that they belong to a culture of their own, a professional aristocracy or guild made up of young writers like themselves and their instructors. This culture has very little, if any, connection with American society in general. It is extremely doubtful, in fact, whether more than a few people outside the universities are aware of its existence. Yet it provides these writers with some of the same supports traditionally provided writers by a loyal readership or, as happened for a time in the 1920s, by an expatriate community of sympathetic peers. And it actually functions as a substitute for both in the case of those of its members whose work fails to attract the attention of that commercial literary world represented by the celebrity maps of *Esquire*.

The process by which a young writer is selected for membership in this culture is relatively simple, but the rewards of selection can be very considerable. If his qualifying manuscripts—consisting usually of a few short stories or poems—are judged by his mentors to be sufficiently promising to earn him admission to a graduate writing program, his status and security as a writer will be assured for an indefinite time to come. He will be placed in close association with other apprentices in workshop sessions in which his and their work will be closely examined and collectively discussed. If he wins acceptance in the classroom and among his peers and instructors, he will become part of a complex network of in-group patronage through which he will be given access to important career opportunities.

His first novel, collection of short stories, or book of poems—any one of which is the customary written requirement for completion of the MFA degree—may be recommended by his instructors for publication by a small press, perhaps staffed in part by former MFA students, or his manuscript may be entered in one or more of the many literary prize contests that are open to young writers and often are judged by a panel of older writers, some of whom may be friends of his instructors. He will in addition be eligible to join the traveling circuit of young writers who, with their instructors, move from one writers' conference to another during the summers, meeting with and listening to other young writers give public readings from their work. It may happen also that one of his instructors, Mr. A., will at some point call an old conference or reading-circuit friend, Mr. B., who is teaching writing at another university, and arrange for the young writer to give a reading at

B.'s university, in exchange for which B. or one of his students will be invited by A. to give a reading at A.'s university.

Before very long, if he has contrived to give readings at the right places and has won favor with the right people, it is quite possible for the young writer to become well known, even slightly famous, on the traveling circuit and to have acquired a supportive audience of his fellow students, his instructors, and their friends without having published much of anything and while remaining entirely unknown to the general reading public. What has happened is that he has become a respectable member of a professional fraternity made up of those who are students and teachers of writing and whose principal means of support consists of one another. Their function is to serve and preserve at all costs the study and teaching of writing, which like any corporate enterprise must be kept going because the survival of its employees depends upon it. Only in a very few exceptional cases are they impelled or sufficiently gifted to resign from the fraternity and make individual reputations in the larger literary world through the creation of a significant body of work. In fact, status within the fraternity serves as a convenient substitute for that kind of achievement and offers its own rewards to the many who would not be capable of it. Among the most tangible of those rewards for the young writer is of course the opportunity to go forth from the university, equipped with his MFA, and be hired by another university to teach even younger young writers how to write.

The writers who belong to this highly politicized fraternity of writing instruction are the academic equivalents of those whose names have become familiar as a result of favorable reviews and publishers' promotion, who may have achieved mention on an *Esquire* map, and yet do not have secure reputations in the literary world. The two groups are comparable in that each has won some status without attaining real position and for reasons of in-group support rather than strong individual accomplishment. Yet the members of the latter group have, for the most part, made some small mark outside the walls of academe and are at least competing with one another to gain recognition and readership for their work.

The academic group of course share this same ambition, but their ambition can so often be too easily tranquilized by the surrogate gratifications offered by their membership in the fraternity, and this can cause them to put off indefinitely the struggle which for any writer is finally the only important struggle—to come to grips with his talent within the stresses and frustrations of the literary marketplace.

The point obviously is that the academic writer is allowed to remain aloof from that struggle for so long as he continues to function within the benevolent precincts of the fraternity and finds an attentive audience, at least for public readings from his work within the fraternity. He need not take the larger risks that writers have traditionally always taken to achieve a hearing for their work because he already has a hearing any time he wants it without taking any risks at all.

In fact, his academic training as a writer will undoubtedly have taught him early on that the taking of risks is decidedly not the gateway to literary success in the fraternity world. In his workshop sessions with his fellow students he will have learned that critical opinion on a particular manuscript is arrived at by consensus, and that critical approval is determined by the number of favorable opinions offered by the class. A piece of writing marked by originality of style or point of view or that does not conform to what is considered fashionable as measured by its resemblance to the work of certain admired mentors such as Raymond Carver or Ann Beattie will undoubtedly be disturbing to many members of the class and so will not be deemed acceptable. Thus, as a result of the democratized process by which critical decisions are reached in the workshop, distinctions are washed out or considered taboo, while a uniformity or homogenization of effects is made to seem a cardinal virtue. One hears more perceptive students complain that after a collective workshop critique, a story or poem will all too often have been denuded of individual character and made to seem anonymous or the product of just anybody or nobody. And it would follow from this that after such an indoctrination a young writer would hardly be disposed to take risks, since his success is measured in the degree of his refusal to take them.

Interestingly enough, this may help to explain the rather astounding absence of critical discussion and debate at the typical public readings that are a regular feature of the program at writers' conferences and the graduate schools of creative writing. So much of the material read on such occasions is so bland, so competently but unexcitingly written, so interchangeable in style and substance that it very seldom stimulates a distinct response from the audience or provides any firm basis for discussion or dispute. Yet, strangely and with an effect that is sometimes eerie, the atmosphere at these readings tends to be downright reverential, as if an awesome spiritual epiphany were taking place, as if the reader on the platform were performing some sacred priestly ritual. And of course that is exactly what he is doing. Through his appearance he is sanctifying the holy function of the writer, and while he is on the platform he is serving as a symbol of the writer in the abstract receiving the adoring attention of the public. He therefore becomes a symbol in turn of all the aspiring writers in the audience and of their own consuming ambition to be the recipients of the same attention. In worshipping him, in other words, they are in effect worshipping themselves and paying homage to the sacramental importance that they attribute to the role of the writer, in preparation for which, after all, they have expended such a large portion of their youth and energy.

This may be a reason why the work being read never seems to be judged on its quality, why there tends to be no discussion of it, and why, in fact, the audience, having heard it read, seems immediately to forget all about it rather in the way they appear to forget the work of the more successful writers whom they profess to admire but also seem never to discuss. For what finally counts in the fraternity system of values is not the quality of the work produced but the continued existence and promotion of writers. Any question raised about quality would surely be considered a form of treason or self-sabotage, since it would threaten to expose one's own grave limitations and might ultimately undermine the system altogether. Hence, it would appear that the members of the fraternity have made an unspoken agreement not to discuss the quality of the work being read by the writer on the platform. That is their insurance against the day when they themselves will be up there reading and will expect to receive unqualified approbation from the audience, not critical judgment.

What is at issue here is a professional fraternity so obsessed with turning out writers that it has lost all regard for the purpose they are supposed to serve and the skill with which they may be expected to serve it. It is rather as if the medical profession were to produce physicians whose ability to treat patients is considered irrelevant when weighed against the fact that the medical profession must be kept going and that the training of physicians is a vital source of revenue and prestige.

But much of the fault is obviously inherent in the premise

on which creative writing programs base their function. It might be argued that while universities may be adequate institutions for the study of literature, they are clearly not constituted to train its potential creators, especially given the nature of the training provided. Unlike graduate programs in the visual arts or in music composition, writing programs do not, as a rule, require their students to learn specific techniques, nor do they measure their progress through their growing ability to make use of those techniques in their own work. There is, in short, no formal curricular plan for monitoring the development of writing students as they evolve from apprenticeship through ever more demanding performance requirements until they arrive at a condition at least approaching competence. Writing students are accepted for training on the basis of such signs of creative promise as may be visible in their qualifying manuscripts, and from then on their work is judged on its own terms, that is, on qualities already present in it at the time they entered training. These qualities may be refined after years of practice in the craft of writing, but they are not enriched by instruction in traditional literary techniques or a close study of the work of acknowledged masters in the field—on the theory, perhaps, that such study might sully the originality of the students. As a result, it is entirely possible for a young writer to be graduated from one of these programs in almost total ignorance of the tradition of his craft and, for that matter, with only a superficial knowledge of literature. He will have retained throughout his training the immature approach to writing with which he began. He may have acquired a certain technical proficiency, but he is unlikely to have developed an individual style or a distinctive point of view, since so much of his time has been spent working in an intellectual vacuum, alone with his manuscripts and unnurtured by any important knowledge beyond the limited experience he had accumulated up to the time he began his studies. He may have learned what he is natively capable of doing as a writer, but not what he *should* be capable of doing now that he has completed his training. For he has not been required to master a series of specific requirements that might have helped him to measure his creative growth and his future creative potential. It is, therefore, not surprising that he would be reluctant to submit his work to critical scrutiny, for his work would be most unlikely to hold up under such scrutiny. Besides, criticism would not only put to the test his abilities as a writer but raise serious questions about the value of the system that supposedly trained him to become one.

But behind the existing deficiencies in the academic training of writers looms the ultimate problem, one so laden with the weight of potential sabotage that one scarcely dares to speak its name. It is that far too many are called to become students of writing and, given the recruiting zeal of the writing programs, far, far too many are chosen. This is not, however, a matter entirely of uncontrolled bureaucratic greed, for in fairness it should be said that many of the applicants for admission to these programs clearly do seem to be promising, at least when judged on the basis of their qualifying manuscripts. Yet too often the promise they show is of the variety most young people show up to the age of about twenty-five, while other qualities far more essential to the continued productivity of writers are not so immediately detectable. There is no way of knowing, for example, that the promising student will possess the kind of obsessive drive to write, or the subject matter to write about, that will keep him functioning for a lifetime. The sad result in too many cases is that writing students will be led by the initial encouragement they receive to spend wasted years trying to become writers when they really do not have the required abilities. What one in fact observes in the majority of writing students is brightness and eagerness, perhaps a certain creative flair, and a religious regard for the holy office of the writer. But rarely do they strike one as having the qualities of mind and spirit that make for excellence. Most of them appear to be nice, well-adjusted, rather conventional, not particularly literary young people who might be equally competent as students of law or dentistry and, therefore, should by all means *be* students of law or dentistry.

It would appear that the writing programs have not yet devised a way to reproduce or incorporate into their curricula the conditions that are best suited to the creation of writers. While it is perfectly true that clonal fabrications of writers proliferate in these programs at an astounding rate, the outlook for their future success remains uncertain. But as some signs already indicate, the future for many of them may hold little more than the production of small, sleek, clonal fabrications of literature.

Part of the problem is that most real writers have already been formed psychologically to become writers long before they are old enough to enter a program. At some time in childhood or early adolescence they will have learned to live with the fact that somehow they are different from others, that there is a detached and perversely watchful ingredient in their natures that causes them to stand just outside those experiences to which their contemporaries so robustly and mindlessly give themselves. Without always being aware of it, writers reenact over and over again, each in his own way, that poignant moment when Mann's Tonio Kröger looks on at the dance and half-despises, half-envies the happy people who are totally and unself-consciously caught up in what they are doing. But the envy in their case as in Kröger's gives way to a superior sense of being the sole custodians of judgment and prophecy, perceiving the scene and foretelling the rest, and knowing that they alone through their artistry will be able to give it a coherence and meaning quite beyond the comprehension of the participants. So the writer becomes a witness and an incurable isolate, doing his work alone and in secret, and being in the end not only fully aware of his otherness but coming to coddle and cultivate it because it forms the perspective necessary to his imaginative re-creation of life.

Behind his knowledge is pride and a feeling that, like the boy in Joyce's "Araby," he is struggling to bear the chalice of his art and otherness safely "through a throng of foes"—those foes being as always the average, the orthodox, the sanctimonious, and the collective. Therefore, a sanctimonious community of writers would be repugnant to him because his entire relation to reality is defined by his productive isolation from community. Perhaps only when he is successful can he view other writers as acceptable fellow workers in the field, but even then the association is strained and laced with suspicion. For he defines himself in relation to them in the way that he defines himself in relation to community—by his difference from them, by the extent to which they do not share his vision of the world and do not intrude upon his imaginative territory but keep within the boundaries of their own.

It is conceivable that at the outset a writing program might give him temporary reassurance that there are others like himself, but again only to strengthen his conviction finally that no one is like himself, no one sees or writes as he does. If, as a result of workshop experiences in which critical judgments are arrived at by consensus and his work is criticized for being original, this conviction is called into question, then his ability to function as he must will gradually be eroded until, if he fails to escape in time, he may well come to share the fate of James's Isabel Archer who, for all her fastidious idealism and determination to lead a superior life, ends in her marriage to Osmond by being "ground in the very mill of the conventional."

Of course by capitulating to that fate he will probably become eligible to join the fraternity of academic writers and may even be invited to give a reading from his work before an audience of his fellows, who will now have no reason not to listen respectfully to his words and applaud him with the greatest enthusiasm when he is finished.

▪ III ▪

Their early training in the graduate schools of creative writing may well account, at least in part, for the fact that in their subsequent careers a surprising number of the newer writers have produced work that is technically conservative, stylistically bland, and often extremely modest in intention, with little about it that could possibly be offensive or provocative or stimulating to anyone. They have been well taught, after all, to avoid taking risks or indulging in the kind of technical experimentation that might provoke an accusation of originality, and to concentrate instead on the slight, safely manageable effect, preferably a briefly rendered, rather wispy moment of experience during which nothing particular happens and out of which arises no large revelation or crescendo of meaning but at most some faint murmur of irony or pity that is often so faint as to be nearly inaudible.

It is a kind of writing, particularly in the shorter form, that bears a very close resemblance to the scenic blips of television, a fact that is not surprising in a generation whose perceptions have been doped and dulled by years of exposure to the electronic anesthesia of that medium. Television projects glimpses of experience as if seen from a train that is moving so fast that the connection of one glimpse to another is impossible to perceive. The glimpses may follow one another in temporal sequence, but it is not a sequence in which meaning is normally accrued or progress is made toward a definitive conclusion. This happens and then this happens and then this happens and then the train disappears into a tunnel and nothing happens. Almost everything that occurs on television is instantly forgettable, and so are most of the stories of, among others, Raymond Carver, Ann Beattie, Jayne Anne Phillips, and Amy Hempel. In each case the memory is given nothing to retain, no form in which the harmonious relation of part to part creates a pattern on which the mind is able to construct a memory.

One obvious explanation for this is that the people and situations so many of these stories concern are too trivial to be remembered. The people are too often shadows without substance, and because so little information about them is provided, they tend to be as indefinable as strangers seen in a snapshot that another stranger has dropped in the street. The situations in which they are presented are also like snapshots, static TV images of ordinary day-to-day life during which strangers exchange fragments of enigmatic conversation while sitting in kitchens drinking beer or driving in shabby cars on the way to someone's ex-spouse's house.

There is no evidence that these experiences are meant to coalesce into drama or so arrange themselves as to produce some climactic insight into a truth about the human condition. They are simply offered as bare minimalist reproductions of a reality so mundane and so completely unilluminated by language or theme that they never become valid subjects for fiction but remain the raw materials for a fiction that is yet to be written. As a rule, no one feature of the depicted experience is given emphasis over another. Everything exists on the same flat plane of inconsequence; hence, no clue is offered as to which element in the action is meant to communicate the meaning of the story—if, indeed, any meaning is intended. As Madison Bell, in a now infamous essay called "Less Is Less," very perceptively observed about the stories of Ann Beattie: "At every important juncture the stories insist on their own lack of depth. . . . In each there is a remarkably skillful accretion of realistic surface detail—beneath which nothing happens. Each, finally, seems to be informed by a sort of polite nihilism."

This effect of nihilism is, in fact, the one element in the stories not only of Beattie but of Carver and the others that leaves any kind of clear impression on the mind. They seem consistently to suggest that human life in general and human experience in particular do not count for very much of anything and are equally consignable to oblivion. Their minimalist technique, furthermore, exactly mirrors this view, its rigid anal retentiveness, its paucity of evaluative nuance reaffirming in constipated language and empty gestures the point made by the authorial monotone: that there is very little to be said for or about people because they and their lives are so utterly inconsequential. And if the stories convey the impression that there is nothing beneath the realistic surfaces of the action, the reason is that in fact there is nothing.

This is perhaps the most important respect in which these writers may be said to betray a connection with the negativism that pervaded and energized so much of classic modernist literature and that remains alive in the work of many of their older contemporaries. But it is a negativism that, in their expressions of it, seems generated in a vacuum. It is not a response to, nor does it represent an attack on, any specific social or political injustice. It is not offered as an attempt to expose the spiritual bankruptcies of modern culture or as a call for some kind of moral reform. In fact, a startling characteristic of such writing is that it expresses absolutely no discernible attitude of any kind toward society as a whole, no critical consciousness of the nature or quality of the milieu in which its characters carry on their insignificant lives. Physical and social environment scarcely exists in the background of the depicted action and appears to have nothing to do with influencing the feelings or the behavior of those involved in the action. Yet the deathly atmosphere of *The Waste Land* overlies everything even as it exists entirely in isolation and without the kind of support provided by the generative context of Eliot's poem. There at least we learned what it was that had died and what was needed to bring about its regeneration. For these writers it would seem that it is not human dignity or religious belief or social justice that has lost meaning but, as I have said, life itself, which is plainly no longer worth living and very nearly no longer worth writing about.

All this would appear to suggest that two important modernist developments have effectively come to an end in the work of these writers: the great tradition of realistic protest sustained in large part by the cultural estrangement of most of the writers involved, and the equally great tradition of technical innovation and experiment that, from Joyce and Eliot to Pynchon, Gaddis, and DeLillo, produced the imperial and apocalyptic poem and novel of rich intellectual complexity and that embodied the ambitious view that literary works can and should become artistic microcosms of a whole society or the modern world. All that visibly remains of the influence of these traditions on the newer writers is the aforementioned negativism of attitude that has no specified meaning or object and a severely delimited realism that is also nonreferential, that is not used in the service of any idea about the nature of human experience or society but simply to express vague feelings of futility.

One explanation for this may be that, unlike most of their predecessors, these writers are not only not estranged from their culture but seem to have no impression of or relation to it at all. In fact, they show no symptoms of having social or intellectual interests of any kind or any sense of belonging to a literary tradition. Above all, they appear never to have possessed the traditional desire of writers to be as original and as completely different from one another as possible. Perhaps because of the homogenizing influence of their training in the creative writing schools, they seem virtually interchangeable, and any one of their novels and stories might conceivably have been written by almost any one of them. It may be, however, that in their resemblance to one another they have found such strength as they are likely ever to possess. For it has enabled publishers to market their various works as if they were identical, one mass-produced product with the same approved ingredients in every package. "A perfect uniformity," says Madison Bell in his essay, "has become the key to the very successful promotion of this new mainstream . . . fiction. 'Like Type O blood,' reads the back jacket of *Shiloh*, 'Bobbie Ann Mason's fiction can be given to almost everyone.' "

But the problem is that, unlike Type O blood, a fiction that can be given to almost everyone is certain to be invigorating to no one. In fact, many of the stories produced not only by Mason but by some of the other mainstream writers belong to that odd species of bloodless fiction so cherished by the editors of *The New Yorker*, in which, not surprisingly, a great deal of their work has been published. It is a fiction that looks soothingly pretty on the page, can be read without effort, would indeed not nourish, offend, or excite anyone, and is fashionably uniform and without point. For a transfusion of real vitality one needs to look to those creative differences and originalities of talent that seem, year by year, to diminish in number as the training schools of literary production turn out look-alike writers and a fiction of sleek designer decor.

▪ IV ▪

A significant number of the newer writers are remarkable for the magnitude of their differences from their immediate predecessors, differences that would be altogether praiseworthy if they were symptomatic of a healthy break with the past and the production of fresh and original work. But unfortunately, the evidence appears to indicate precisely the opposite: that these writers continue to be notable more for what they are not than for what they are. Not only do they seem unable or unwilling to take the large imaginative risks required to carry forward the modern experimentalist tradition, but nowhere in their work does one find more than cursory reference to issues that were such a major concern and constituted such a vital topical dimension of the fiction of Pynchon, Vonnegut, Mailer, Heller, Gaddis, and some others of the older literary generation.

Even when these writers were operating in areas well beyond the limits of conventional realism, when they appeared to be offering highly convoluted metaphorical abstractions of actual experience, they still were able to employ these methods to investigate matters that were of the most urgent practical importance to their time and generation. Although Pynchon's novels are indeed highly convoluted and are, if anything, overpoweringly excessive in their preoccupation with realistic detail, they are built on a single topical idea, what is, in fact, a sweeping metaphysical conception of modern history as largely determined by the experience of the two World Wars, events that in Pynchon's view were themselves determined by the workings of a secret but universal conspiracy, the search for the source of which is the motivating obsession of his characters. Vonnegut, on a far less sophisticated level, gave explicit attention in his fiction to a variety of topical issues ranging from the stupidities of war and the prospect of worldwide nuclear annihilation to the corruptive effects of great wealth and power and the pollution of the natural environment.

Mailer's most compelling psycho-social vision was of an American national character paralyzed after the second war by a failure to grow creatively and discover new circuits of consciousness, a failure that on the individual level resulted in the compensatory lust for the promiscuous slaughter of animals that possessed such a character as Rusty Jethroe in *Why Are We in Vietnam?* and that drove us collectively to become involved in the tragedy of that war. Gaddis, in his monumental novel, *JR*, took on a task no less ambitious and topical than the wholesale debasement of the English language by the barbaric invasions of technocratic newspeak and psychobabble, the gibberish jargon of the computer, of Wall Street finance and multimedia education, which have served to sever the connection that is supposed to exist between words and the realities they are intended to describe.

Even earlier, in *Catch-22*, Heller made a very similar satirical assault on the bureaucratic doublethink language of the military, while through his portrait of Bob Slocum in *Something Happened*, he dramatized the dilemma of a professionally successful contemporary man whose feelings of personal and cultural loss in an affluent world of privilege are maddening just because he can find no language to describe them satisfactorily and no causal basis for them in objective fact.

These writers of course had the advantage over their younger contemporaries of having lived through a period of history in which certain crucial events and conditions—the Depression, the second war, the anti-Communist hysteria of the Eisenhower-McCarthy era, the imminence of nuclear holocaust—touched and disrupted their personal lives. It is therefore not surprising that they should have become aware of a strong symbiotic relationship between their individual experience and the developing macrocosm of contemporary history, or that they should seek to confront in their work some of the most important and painful realities of the history they have lived through and survived.

Their younger contemporaries, by contrast, show no evidence in their fiction that they perceive such a relationship, and that may well account, at least in part, for the fact that such events as do occur in their stories and novels seem to occur without relation to any discernible context or consciousness of history. It is as if, where their predecessors took the position of embattled and often outraged critics of the conditions of their time, these writers are either oblivious to such conditions or have achieved some form of peaceful accommodation with them.

One possible explanation is that as members or slightly younger siblings of the sixties generation, these writers came to maturity and continue to exist in a relative intellectual and political vacuum, a period of history when most of the issues about which that generation professed to feel most passionately had turned out to be either settled by the end of the Vietnam War or perhaps were from the beginning bankrupt in substance. This is to suggest that there was always a large dimension of self-deception and downright speciousness about the entire sixties activist movement, a fact that may account for the dramatic suddenness with which, in the seventies and eighties, so many of its members embraced the most materialistic values of the Establishment they once considered their vicious enemy. But the most militant crusaders of the time now appear to have been most notable for the curiously abstract nature of their zeal for reform, which is to say that they seemed to be demonstrating in the name of largely *theoretical* constructs of issues rather than the concrete specifics of issues. And one supposes that they were doing so because they lacked direct personal experience of those issues, because they were precisely as detached from the world in which those issues concretely existed as they were from the ugly realities of their social environment.

It could in fact be argued that their activism was the result more of ideological sentimentality than of direct personal frustration and suffering, and perhaps that is why they clung to it with such intensity—because it was what they had instead of personal involvement, because it was a structure of quasi-commitment that had behind it all the appearances of vigorous feeling without having been derived from vigorous feeling, and so was their only means of confronting experience in a dynamic and dramatic way. They were very probably the first American generation of rebels not to have suffered to some degree personally as a result of the injustices and inequities they sought to eradicate, and this served to create a crippling separation between their professed principles and their felt emotions, between their official radicalism and their practical understanding. If they had ever actually been victims of privation or persecution, if they had ever known the ugliness of discrimination, lived among the poor of Appalachia or Harlem, gone hungry, fought in a war, or tried to survive under Soviet or Chinese communism, they might have found a living basis for their outrage and discovered the terms for an effective personal rebellion. They might also have found a corrective for their tendency to romanticize the poor and downtrodden as well as the joys of life in a socialist republic. But middle-class affluence, American citizenship, and their favored or, from their point of view, unfavored position in history deprived them of these experiences and so left them physically and psychologically isolated from the objects of their programmatic compassion and anger, theoretical in their concern for other people's painful realities.

With such an ideologically impoverished background, it follows that so many of the newer writers should seem oblivious to the larger historical issues that so profoundly preoccupied their predecessors. But they also seem remarkably oblivious to the realities of social context and physical milieu in general. They do not indicate in their work that they are aware of the ugliness and vapidity of the contemporary urban and suburban environment. They take no critical attitude toward it. It does not provoke them to raise qualitative questions about it—like those, for example, that Mailer, Vonnegut, Gaddis, Pynchon, and Heller have all been provoked to raise—but as is the case with their response to social issues, they appear to perceive it, if at all, as an abstraction or as an entirely neutral medium, as natural and invisible as the air they breathe. In the K Mart fiction of Bobbie Ann Mason and Frederick Barthelme—to take two notable instances—the environment typified by the K Mart is not evaluated as the sleazy and soul-deadening thing it is. It is treated simply as a blank space where the action occurs, as a featureless corridor through which the characters move in their unimpeded progress toward inconsequence.

One might suppose that if Mason, Barthelme, and their contemporaries had ever found themselves in conflict with a strongly resistant environment or had been exposed to any of the older, more provincial, and more readily engageable forms of social confrontation—with the small town or neighborhood of fifty or sixty years ago, with authoritarian pre-Spock parents or overly strict discipline at school—they might have found their environment real and the question of its quality crucial just because they existed in a state of constant opposition to it and suffered within it, as Joyce suffered in and so found real the life of Dublin and Thomas Wolfe the small town life of the South. But it is difficult to imagine how one can confront or resist an environment that puts up no resistance, that is open, bland, uniform, monotonous, and at the same time smoothly functional and accommodative like that of a modern housing development or shopping mall. All one can do with either, besides live badly in it, is find it too dull and depressing to be noticed. If a person has grown up in a development and shopped his whole life in a mall—and in this country over the last thirty years a child of the middle classes could scarcely have avoided that calamity—it would not be surprising if his sensibilities were as atrophied as the optic nerves of fish spawned for centuries in caves.

Thus, in their isolation from the larger social issues of their time and their apparent blindness to their environment, these writers seem, on the evidence of their work, to be left with one essential subject, the personal life, a subject that of course has always been a major preoccupation of the novel and an immensely valuable one, particularly in those instances when it has been presented in the form of a dramatic conflict between the emotional needs of the individual and the moral imperatives imposed by his society. But over and over again in their fiction these writers tend to treat the personal life as if it were a phenomenon existing totally apart from society and without connotations that would give it meaningful relevance to a general human condition or dilemma—in the sense, for example, that Heller's Yossarian or Vonnegut's Billy Pilgrim become representative both of human types and of problems shared by an entire generation.

The reason for this should be obvious: Because these writers are defective in their responses to their historical position, they are unable to perceive their characters as responding to particular historical forces. The characters in the fiction of Carver, Beattie, Hempel, Barthelme, and some of their contemporaries may be closely observed; the minutiae of their daily existence may be described in considerable detail. But they tend to be seen from the outside, not created from within, which is to say that they are not brought imaginatively to life but remain comatose figures who exist at all solely by virtue of the factual details accumulated around them.

Perhaps in an effort to compensate for this deficiency, a number of these writers have chosen to become minimalists, a role that both compounds and helps to conceal the problem of giving some larger significance to personal life, since the minimalist technique imposes the requirement that less be said at the same time that it can avoid revealing that less is all there is to be said.

Still another method of compensating is to concentrate, in the portrayal of character, on those aspects of behavior that are bizarre, eccentric, arbitrary, or shockingly unexpected and are, as horror fiction demonstrates, always dependable, if superficial, sources of dramatic interest. Those who resort to this method—and Jayne Anne Phillips, T. Coraghessan Boyle, and Bob Shacochis come to mind as being among its most accomplished practitioners—are thus able to avoid the problem of making character meaningful. All that is necessary is that it be arrestingly strange.

But regardless of the kind of compensation employed, the

dimension of the deficiency it is designed to conceal becomes evident in an area where no compensation is sufficient, and that is the area in which the fiction of these writers fails again and again to achieve dramatic climax and resolution. It may be most artfully composed. The characters may be described in the greatest detail, or, as is the case in minimalist fiction, only superficially. But their actions and interactions do not build toward that magical moment when the reader senses that developing dramatic tensions have somehow achieved release in the serenity of understanding. What one repeatedly finds instead is that such tensions as have been generated either fail to find release or are dissipated in a fog of ambiguity, which, more often than not, is an affectation of profundity to cover a failure of conception. One is left, in short, with an apparently fictionalized fragment of experience that is, in fact, not fictionalized because it has no thematic significance. What characterizes such fiction is that it never finds its end in its beginning; it simply begins and stops.

There is undoutedly much truth in the observation Christopher Lasch makes in *The Minimal Self* that contemporary lives consist of "isolated acts and events." They have "no story, no pattern, no structure as an unfolding narrative." Therefore, a literature that seeks to reflect those lives accurately will have as its defining features "an immersion in the ordinary . . . a rejection of clarifying contexts that show relationships among objects or events, a refusal [or an inability] to find patterns of any kind, an insistence on the random quality of experience."

However, such a literature, regardless of the accuracy with which it *reflects* contemporary reality, is also a literature guilty of succumbing to what was once known, in a more critically scrupulous time, as the imitative fallacy. A mirror held up to nature may give back a true reflection, but it is, after all, only a reflection. In T. S. Eliot's phrase, it "ends its course in the desert of exact likeness to the reality which is perceived by the most commonplace mind," while what is wanted in literature is a reality perceived, understood, and imaginatively transformed by an extraordinary mind.

CHAPTER II

LESS IS A LOT LESS

In *The Great Tradition*, during his notorious and not altogether fair assessment of *Heart of Darkness*, F. R. Leavis charged Joseph Conrad with a form of adjectival fakery. He argued that Conrad was not content to allow his brilliantly evoked dramatic instances of horror and perversion to make his point but felt obliged to resort to "an adjectival and worse than supererogatory insistence on 'unspeakable rites,' 'unspeakable secrets,' 'monstrous passions,' 'inconceivable mystery' and so on . . . that is merely an emotional insistence on the presence of what he can't produce. [Conrad] is intent on making a virtue out of not knowing what he means."

While the majority of the newer writers most emphatically cannot be accused of adjectival insistence, if only because they tend to insist that nothing is worthy of insistence, adjectival or otherwise, they nevertheless do tend to write about situations that often seem extremely weighty with portent, that almost visibly ache for release into climax or revelation, but then over and over again fail to achieve it. One imagines that, like most of us, they have experienced or conceived of moments in life that appeared, on the face of it, to promise some dramatic yield, some significant wisdom about the human condition, *if only* they could determine precisely what that wisdom was. But then, instead of waiting for the revelation to dawn, they write the experience into a piece of fiction, perhaps hoping that through the sacramental act of writing the meaning will epiphanize without their even knowing what it was.

A less charitable hypothesis might be that they learned in the MFA writing programs that very often when such underdone fiction was presented during a workshop session, the students assumed that a profound meaning was contained somewhere within it but that they were too stupid to perceive it. They therefore were inclined to praise the work without in the least understanding it rather than take the risk of exposing themselves as stupid. Thus, failure to achieve meaning becomes widely and enthusiastically recognized by the timid as extreme subtlety of meaning.

The late Raymond Carver is commonly considered to be the major influence in popularizing this kind of fiction and making it a virtue for a writer not to know what he means. Carver wrote, often very gracefully, about people who seem perpetually on the edge of disaster and who do not have far to fall because they are people wholly without talents, ambitions, or prospects drifting aimlessly wherever the poor are out of work together, while burdened by alcohol, divorce, and a depression of spirit that cannot quite speak its name. Carver wrote with a curious kind of throttled intensity about these people and gained much of his special quality from what he did not say about them, what he left out of his account of their characters and situations.

In this respect he, along with writers like Joan Didion, Ann Beattie, and Donald and Frederick Barthelme, may be said to be the contemporary progenitors of the minimalist method, in which what is barely stated about a person or an experience is given a kind of subaqueous luminescence as well as a certain air of menacing fatality by the materials that are left out but the presence of which is nevertheless hauntingly *there,* lurking just behind the venetian blinds of the shuttered prose. The ghostly presence of the eliminated is absolutely vital to the successful minimalist effect. But it is essential to know whether there is material that has been eliminated or material that is simply absent. The distinction is crucial and is perhaps best illustrated by the example of Hemingway, the minimalist Papa of them all. His famous short story, "A Clean, Well-Lighted Place," is conventionally cited as a piece of highly effective minimalist fiction, and it is so in large part because in planning the story Hemingway composed, but in the actual writing omitted, several elaborately detailed histories of the characters, even of the soldier and the girl who are briefly seen as they pass in the street outside the café. Although Hemingway failed to use this material, its presence is felt throughout and is largely responsible for generating the tone of just barely suppressed anguish that is the dominant effect not only here but in the most successful Hemingway stories.

The old man, who is a frequent late-night patron of the café, has lost his wife and has recently attempted suicide. He drinks steadily until he is drunk but never shows that he is. The younger of the two waiters is impatient for him to leave because he is anxious to go home to bed with his wife. The older waiter is more sympathetic because, like the old man, he himself has no one to go home to and knows what the old man feels. But even when he rewrites in his mind The Lord's Prayer and substitutes the word *nada* for many of the nouns and verbs, the older waiter does not give himself up to the despair represented by what he is doing, nor will he acknowledge that it is this despair that will keep him awake until daylight. "After all, he said to himself, it is probably only insomnia. Many must have it."

The older waiter and the old man are thus joined by their

common commitment to a dignified forbearance, which in the Hemingway lexicon of human virtue is the most admirable form of moral courage. The two men are careful not to display their true emotions in public (the older waiter even denies that they exist), for to do so would be unseemly. Yet those emotions are struggling for expression just beneath the surface of the story, and the fact that they are held in check by those most tormented by them is the perfect dramatic analogue for the full knowledge of them and their causes that Hemingway possessed but also quite deliberately held in check.

Like the characters in this story the protagonists of Hemingway's best fiction are well suited by temperament and experience to be compatible with the stylistic premises of the minimalist method. They are all men whose traumatic histories have rendered them incapable of responding to a wider range of sensory impressions than the Hemingway prose is able to record. They cannot allow themselves to be placed in situations that might threaten to "rush their sensations" or cause them to experience a dangerous excess of feeling that might lead to the collapse of sanity into violent disorder or even madness. Decorous behavior along a few carefully chosen channels of activity is at all times essential to their survival, and the prose in which they are presented is the precise verbal equivalent of their extremely fragile relationship to reality.

Gertrude Stein, in one of her better-known pronouncements on Hemingway, said that there is a real story to be told about him, one that he should write himself, "not those he writes but the confessions of the real Ernest Hemingway." Clearly, Hemingway did not write it and could not because, as his protagonists indicate, the real story was too deeply disturbing to tell, just as the young Nick Adams could not bring himself to enter the shadowy part of the Big Two-Hearted River where it ran into the swamp—because "in the swamp fishing was a tragic adventure." But the remarkable fact is that in telling as much or as little of the story as he did, Hemingway managed through his complex minimalist artistry to use words in such a way that we are allowed to see past them and to glimpse the outlines of the mysterious and probably tragic adventure that the words were not quite able to describe but were also not quite able to conceal.

In Raymond Carver's fiction the real story, such as it is, appears to be what is on the page, and there is no evidence that more might have been said than the minimalist language implies but refuses to say. If, as Hemingway once observed about his own use of understatement, "the dignity of movement of an iceberg is due to only one-eighth of it being above water," then Carver's work clearly lacks that kind of dignity, for the portion showing above the surface appears to be the entire iceberg. While his method can and often does generate an effect of ominous foreboding, of things just on the verge of falling into chaos, it is more an effect of impending physical or financial disaster than of psychological breakdown.

Part of the problem is that Carver's characters are so meagerly developed, so little information about them is given, that one has no knowledge of their history or their psychological condition beyond the fact that they are depressed by alcoholism, unemployment, or divorce. One, therefore, has no sense that a symbiotic relationship exists between the minimalist method and the need of the characters to function and feel in a minimalist manner. That obviously is the key to the success of Hemingway's use of the method: What his language withholds is what his characters are unable emotionally to confront.

Carver's people, by contrast, show no evidence of suffering from that kind of fragility. Except for the shroud of chronic dispiritedness that hangs over them, they do not seem responsive to much of anything, and not because they wish to avoid dangerous emotions but because they appear not to have emotions. And inevitably, since they are so thinly drawn as characters, there is no effective way of distinguishing their point of view from Carver's. Their failure of response becomes his own, and his minimalist method comes to seem not a statement of the little he deliberately chose to say out of all he might have said but rather a confession that this is all he had to say, perhaps because his characters are simply not interesting or important enough to deserve extended development or because he was unable to take full imaginative possession of them.

These difficulties are most clearly revealed in those early sketches or vignettes that first brought Carver to the attention of the reading public and caused some normally discriminating critics to hail him as a new master of the short story form. In the piece called "Gazebo," for example, a man and his wife, who seem recently to have become managers of a motel, have locked themselves in a suite and drink whiskey while they discuss the breakdown of their marriage. In the motel office the telephone keeps ringing. Potential customers pound on the door, blow their car horns, and finally drive off in disgust when no one responds. It appears that the husband has had a purely sexual affair with the Mexican maid who has been working for them. The wife has found out, and now everything is falling apart—the job, which, since the wife's discovery, they have badly neglected, and the life they have had together.

The husband does not know why he had relations with the maid. It was something he simply fell into because the woman just happened to be in a room cleaning while he was replacing a washer in a bathroom faucet. The next thing he knew they were down on the bed. As is the case with so many of Carver's characters, his action is purely impulsive and arbitrary. It does not come as the result of developing discord or frustration between him and his wife. In fact, he tells us that they have had a very good marriage, and the motel job, which has now been destroyed, had apparently promised them a new start after some years of occupational drift. The infidelity also does not provide insight except into the typical failure of Carver's people to put up any resistance of will or to exercise any power of choice over the conduct of their lives. They simply float in listlessness as the couple have floated from job to job, and life takes destructive charge of them. Hence, there is no revelation of meaning or character and no dramatic substance to be found in the husband's affair. What is finally revealed is moral inertia rather than the tragic defeat that might have resulted if the couple had not been emotionally empty and if one could know from what higher level of happiness or success, if any, the event had fatally dislodged them. The whole thing simply happened, and while that may be true of the way events sometimes do occur in life, contingency is an impotent substitute for motive in fiction.

Carver's effort to achieve significance through the image of the gazebo in the concluding section of the story also proves to be impotent. The wife in her misery recalls a time when she and her husband were driving in the country and stopped at a farmhouse to ask for a drink of water. The old people who owned the farm showed them around the place.

> And there was this gazebo there out back. . . . And the woman said that years before, I mean a real long time ago, men used to come around and play music out there on a Sunday, and the people would sit and listen.

> I thought we'd be like that too when we got old enough. Dignified. And in a place. And people would come to our door.

Carver obviously intended this pastoral recollection to suggest what it is that the couple may have lost with the disintegration of their love and marriage. But it is actually specious, sentimental, and dramatically unearned, first, because the wife is projecting onto the old people a value they may or may not have really represented. They may, after all, have achieved their alleged dignity by living lives of wholly unimaginative and dogged respectability, or they may in fact have achieved it through the exercise of real moral courage and rectitude. But the point is that whichever was the case, neither has anything to do with the wife and her husband who have done nothing to take command of their lives and have no resources that might have achieved suitable symbolic representation in the poignant image of the gazebo. They are, have always been, and presumably always will be destined to be without a place where people might come to the door.

Some of Carver's stories are artistically more successful than "Gazebo" and represent departures from the alcoholism–marital breakdown formula that has made so many others of his seem monotonously repetitive and quickly forgettable. These more ambitious stories tend to remain longer in the memory, but their tenure there is by no means secure because they so often contain elements that, when considered separately, seem promising but when put together somehow fail to ignite into revelation.

In "The Third Thing That Killed My Father Off," for example, the central character, a man called Dummy because he is deaf and seldom speaks, stocks his pond with bass, then puts up an electrified fence to keep people from fishing for them. A flood carries away the fish, and Dummy, whose wife is evidently unfaithful, kills her and drowns himself in the pond. The young narrator's father tells him that "that's what the wrong kind of woman can do to you, Jack." But then Jack says, "I don't think Dad really believed it. I think he just didn't know who to blame or what to say."

With the father's interpretation declared untrustworthy, we are left with certain details that, taken together, might constitute a plausible explanation for Dummy's behavior. The wife has presumably been unfaithful to him for years, and it may be that possession of the fish has helped him to live with the fact since they represent something he can keep to himself and protect from the incursions of others. When the fish are lost, he is left with nothing of his own, and so is driven to commit murder and suicide. But the problem with this is that because of Carver's extremely minimalist treatment of Dummy, who, after all, is deaf and nearly speechless, the man is virtually invisible as a character. All we know about him is what Jack's father and Jack himself observe, and what they give us is a set of bare facts, at best the information necessary for a possible psychological profile or a case history. But information of this kind is clearly not characterization but rather a way of compelling the reader to do the writer's imagining for him, in this instance to create from the few known facts a character for Dummy that is not actually created in the story.

One infers from the responses of many younger readers of Carver that one source of his appeal for them is the seeming ease with which he achieves his effects. Therefore, unlike Faulkner, Joyce, or Pynchon, he does not cow them by the power of his genius into feeling inferior. On the contrary, they often seem to feel that this is something they can quite readily imagine themselves doing in their own writing. But if one looks closely at his work, what appears to be an effortless mastery is frequently revealed to be the result of an extremely modest intention. Carver is very careful not to try what he believes he cannot easily achieve. But the fact that he is not always able to achieve even his modest intentions may indicate that there is considerably less here than meets the eye.

Even in the stories that seem comparatively successful—"So Much Water So Close To Home," for example, or "A Small, Good Thing"—there is again evidence of a thinness of conception and opaqueness of execution that, to be sure, are often almost concealed by the apparently effortless grace of the writing. Yet there is also an air of bleakness about these stories that appears to be the result not only of a darkly negative vision of life but of a certain poverty of imagination. It is as if Carver's work came into being against the resistance of an enormous internal pressure to be silent, and this causes his minimalist method to seem to be an expression of the feebleness of his hold on his materials, the verbal index perhaps of some deeply lodged visceral conviction that there is very little of any worth to be said about the sorry state of human existence.

▪ II ▪

That, at any rate, is one likely possibility. Another more charitable to Carver is that, whatever his strengths and weaknesses as a writer, he is to some important degree the product and victim of a social situation that is extremely limited in dramatic potential and in which the resources for the display of depth and complexity, whether of character or relationship, are greatly diminished.

This may be a significant reason why the short story has become the dominant fictional form of the present time. It is not merely because of the greatly shortened attention span of the generation of readers brought up on television. What is more to the point is that, if one can judge by the work of some of the current practitioners of the form, we now inhabit a society in which human relations have become increasingly ephemeral and superficial, a society, in fact, of aimless transients who are often held together by nothing more than temporary geographical propinquity and who are perhaps most notable for being as migratory emotionally as they are physically.

To the extent that any literary form is capable of giving adequate expression to the curiously amorphous nature of such a society, it would seem to be the short story. For unlike the novel, which normally depends on the existence of some continuity of relationship among its characters as well as some stability of physical location, the short story—at least in its contemporary version—most often records not relationships but fleeting and sometimes meaningless encounters among people who, even though they may at the moment be living together, are really not together at all but tend to observe one another in a bemused, vaguely distrustful way as if they were scrutinizing strangers on a passing subway train.

Ann Beattie's stories, for example, are often presented from the point of view of a youngish, middle-class woman who is shown to be in some way deranged whether as a cause or an effect of feeling alienated from what is happening around her—or the fact that nothing is happening that she can find real. Such relations as she may have with men are usually in a state of deterioration, partly because the men are churlish and remote and do not talk to her or she to them. Hence, their role in her life seems probationary either by her or their choosing and may at any moment come to an end. Perhaps in compensation, she typically becomes obsessively preoccupied with the small housekeeping details of her physical environment—her potted plants, her pets, her furniture—since they promise to provide the only source of dependability available to her.

But then, interestingly enough, Beattie herself, in her manner of creating her stories, is similarly preoccupied. Her fictional world is in fact one in which very little of significance happens, yet which is so crowded with descriptions of details that the physical environment and physical appearance in general might be said to be her main character. Everything that could possibly attract even one's most cursory attention is minutely described, and Beattie is a brilliant describer, one of the most gifted and imaginative prose writers of her generation. Yet what actually happens again and again in her fiction is that through her remarkable powers of description she almost but not quite succeeds in directing attention away from the emotional emptiness of her characters and in creating the illusion of psychological depth and complexity where in fact none is demonstrated.

Norman Mailer once acutely observed that when the action lapses in a John Updike novel, Updike becomes confused and begins to cultivate his private vice: he *writes.* I once observed that when the action lapses in a Mary McCarthy novel, she starts making lists, and she does this not only because she has momentarily lost the thread of her narrative but apparently because she cannot cope with emotion. Like a shell-shocked Hemingway hero who concentrates on the little rituals of fishing to keep from having to think, McCarthy turns her attention to objects to keep from having to feel. She begins to inventory the furniture, the books on the shelves, or the contents of the kitchen cupboards. As Mailer has said on another occasion, "Lists and categories are always the predictable refuge of the passionless, the timid, and the bowel-bound," and presumably they are so because they are a way of achieving an effect of coherence and security where otherwise one might be obliged to confront the psychological perils of real characterization.

One cannot say for certain that the same is true of Beattie. But one can say with some assurance, given the evidence at hand, that her extraordinarily intense concentration on exteriors does tend to obscure the fact that, whether out of fear of feeling or some deep insensitivity to the way others feel, she seems unable to explore interiors, to reveal the essential and complex humanness of the human beings whose environment she so intricately documents but who are really not seen as human beings at all.

For example, in Beattie's novel, *Chilly Scenes of Winter*, about which I will have more to say later, this passage of intricate documentation is notable for what it does not say about the character, Charles, whose environment is being documented:

> He drives to a store and buys a big package of pork-chops and a bag of potatoes and a bunch of broccoli and a six-pack of Coke. He remembers cigarettes for Sam when he is checking out, in case he's well enough to smoke. He buys a National Enquirer that features a story about Jackie Onassis's face-lift. James Dean is supposed to be alive and in hiding somewhere, too. Another vegetable. Not dead at all. *East of Eden* is one of his favorite films. He saw it, strangely enough, on television after he and Laura went to a carnival and rode on a Ferris Wheel.

There are conceivably three defensible reasons for such preoccupation with trivia. It could be that Beattie wishes to make the point that the environment, both physical and mental, in which her characters move and barely have their being is indeed trivial and she wants to expose it as such. Or she may see environmental details as containing some sort of microcosmic sacramental authenticity, perhaps of the kind William Blake imagined when he saw "a World in a grain of sand, and a Heaven in a wild flower." But in a fictional world of unrelieved and unexamined secularity such as hers, this seems highly unlikely, and Beattie is surely no William Blake.

Finally, it could be she is saying that Charles is barely sentient because he has suffered some unspecified deep trauma and so keeps himself psychically intact by concentrating on the most banal details in order to avoid the perils of higher thought. But the problem is that nowhere in the narrative context does one find evidence to support any of these explanations. There is nothing to indicate that Charles is anything other than rather stupid or that his catatonic condition is not simply his normal mode of dimly relating to reality. Or are we honestly supposed to believe that he perceives only groceries and the news of Jackie Onassis's face-lift because he is so occupied with mooning over his lost love, Laura?

There is, furthermore, nothing in Beattie's narrative tone throughout the novel to indicate that she sees and is condemning either him or his environment as trivial. Rather, she appears to be listing the items he is faintly responding to as if they were the given and perfectly acceptable furnishings of her fictional world.

In some contemporary fiction, to be sure, characters are indeed meaningfully revealed through the kind and quality of the furnishings that surround them. Tom Wolfe was undoubtedly the first to describe the intricate status relationship existing between the brand names of products and the people who own and use them. Also in the fiction of Bret Easton Ellis and Jay McInerney brand names and fashionable places become in themselves characters as finely differentiated in terms of status and taste as any of the characters who find evidence of status and taste through possessing or frequenting them.

But this is clearly not the case in Beattie's world, for it is as if she, along with the several other writers who resemble her in this respect, were presenting environmental details, whether high-fashion brand names or a six-pack of Coke, as if they had no characterizing power of any kind, simply because they are *there,* and she has included them in her fictional repertoire because she does not know what else to do. Every work of fiction, after all, needs to contain some sort of physical and social setting, and, ideally, that setting should exist in some symbiotic or emblematic relationship to the drama of the characters who move through it. But if one sees no such relationship or is incapable of creating one, then supposedly any old setting will do for any old cast of characters. In Beattie's case, however, one becomes mesmerized by the itemized listing of environmental furnishings to the point where one is nearly persuaded that the characters are being created through their relation to the items listed. But then one recognizes that they are not because they have no relation.

But one is forced to admit that the whole question of characterization in much of the new fiction is rather beside the point, since so many of the characters presented are people about whom very little can be said. Very often they are seen only in terms of the fact that they are suffering from various degrees of depression, at times apparently causeless, at other times because they have been involved in failed relationships from the pain of which, like Beattie's Charles, they are in hiding or as a result of which they are able to feel nothing. Over and over again the relationships that have failed are amatory, marital, or parental, and nearly always it is someone other than oneself who is to blame for the failure. Lovers have betrayed one by leaving one.

Women are haunted by the memory of their first husbands as they find themselves drawn passively into relationships with loutish lovers and second husbands. Mother and Father have betrayed their children by getting divorced. Or Mother is destroying the tranquility of the home by dying of cancer or becoming addicted to alcohol or other drugs. Or Father has betrayed Mother as well as the children by taking a homosexual lover. Domestic crisis becomes a substitute for characterization because the only thing a character can do in response to it is to become depressed.

Yet even within the recurrent situations of failed relationship, there is a curious dearth of evidence that a relationship of any depth or significance ever existed. To take again the example of Beattie's Charles, he yearns to be reconciled with the faithless Laura, but the specific justifications for his desire are missing from his soulful memories of their time together—missing, that is, unless one can be persuaded that such preteen dating pastimes as watching *East of Eden* on television together and riding a Ferris Wheel at a carnival are matters deserving to be recalled with the deepest sensations of loss.

But then it seems not to be the quality or even the reality of the relationship that is important to such socially typifying characters as Charles. More to the point is the fact that relationships are seen so often in this fiction not as vital shared experiences but as possessions. This is to say that they represent for the characters what brand-name products and fashionable night spots represent in the novels of Ellis and McInerney: They are symbols of one's status as a human being and proof of one's self-worth in a society in which true emotional commitment is a rare and hazardous undertaking and there are very few other measures of self-worth beyond what one owns, whether it be a lover or a pair of expensive high-fashion shoes.

Thus, if it can be said that when the action lapses in her fiction, Beattie describes, the important issue is that what she describes are the physical furnishings of people who operate on very much the same acquisitive and materialistic premises that may impel her to itemize so obsessively the material details of their world.

But the fact is that the action in her fiction does not exactly lapse. Instead, it becomes bizarre, mysteriously inexplicable, or absurd to the point where, as happens as a result of her physical descriptions, one's attention is at least momentarily diverted from the fact that her characters are not characterized to the colorful strangeness and novelty of their apparently unmotivated behavior.

Representative examples of this effect can be found everywhere in Beattie's fiction, but perhaps the clearest can be found in two stories from her first collection called, accurately enough, *Distortions*.

In "Eric Clapton's Lover" a woman named Beth Fisher has married Franklin because he thought she should since they were both born on the same day in March, two years apart. Unfortunately, they have entirely incompatible tastes in food. "Beth liked *chiles relenos*, Bass ale, gazpacho; Franklin liked mild foods: soufflés, quiche, pea soup." Beth's taste causes her to get fat, and "as she got larger, she got more vehement, less willing to compromise." Things worsen between the couple when their son brings home a new wife who is learning to drive a rig. She sits on the sofa and demonstrates how to turn a truck wheel, and she can talk about nothing else.

After this Beth speaks to Franklin almost not at all. He tries to speak to her, but she does not respond. As a staff member of a magazine, he is promoted one day to the editorship, then he tenders his resignation to become a seller of tickets at a movie theater. He soon leaves that job and goes to live with a Puerto Rican woman whom he has picked up on the street and to whom he is attracted because she is wearing bright orange lipstick. It seems that her one ambition is to become Eric Clapton's lover, but since Clapton is likely not to be available, she settles for Franklin.

Beth in the meantime has become a saleswoman in a department store. When she next sees Franklin, he is sitting in their living room reading a magazine that displays on its cover a lunging shark, "more teeth than body," and "to the side, a man . . . being slugged in the face." Beth and Franklin have little to say to each other. Beth says only that there is "nothing I wanted to say to you and there was nothing I wanted to hear." Franklin spends the night sleeping on the Eames chair, and the next morning they find themselves snowed in. Beth insists that he crumble some bread and go out and feed it to the birds. He does so, and the story ends as follows: " 'It's hard to imagine that somewhere in the world it's warm today,' Beth said, forehead against the foggy window. She was chewing celery, heavily sprinkled with chili powder."

Here there are several instances of gratuitous bizarreness. Beth and Franklin marry simply because they were born on the same day; the son's wife is reduced to the one bare fact that she is learning to drive a rig; Franklin inexplicably leaves his editorial job, becomes a seller of movie tickets, and decides to take as a lover a woman whose sole characterizing logo is the color of her lipstick and her preference for Eric Clapton; Beth decides that Franklin should go out and feed the birds.

All this is pseudocharacterization in the sense that it consists of quaint or cute manifestations of idiosyncrasy that finally reveal nothing about Beth and Franklin but tend, because of their oddity, to conceal the fact that they reveal nothing. Beattie here displays a disturbing tendency to patronize and at the same time manipulate her characters in such a way that they appear to be vaguely comic puppets jerking grotesquely on the strings of her antic imagination. The trouble, however, is that one does not know what reality their performance is intended to dramatize or burlesque, for behind their gyrating movements there appears to be no cohering idea, no rational pattern of conception.

In "Vermont," another and quite different story from *Distortions*, Beattie reminds one a good deal of Carver. There is the toneless, rather catatonic narrative voice that manages to give everything the same significance or gives nothing significance. The characters, uninspected from the inside, are sleepwalking, apparitional. David is married to the unnamed female narrator. They have a small daughter named Beth. A friend of theirs, Noel, lives on the second floor of the high-rise in which they live on the first floor. Noel's wife, Susan, has left him to move in with John, who lives on the eleventh floor. Then a short time later David leaves the narrator. There is no explanation beyond the fact that she and he compete with each other in everything they do—in scuba diving when he always snatches the best shells, at tennis, "precision parking, three-dimensional ticktacktoe, soufflés," and he always wins.

The narrator and Noel begin seeing each other. It occurs to the narrator that David makes her sad and Noel makes her happy, an insight that exactly defines the depth of her understanding of human relationships. She and Noel often have dinner together. At a Chinese restaurant Noel says to the narrator, "You know how you can tell a Chinese restaurant from any other? . . . Even when it's raining, the cats still run for the street."

The narrator and Noel go to visit his friends, Charles and Sol, in Vermont. Charles and Sol are living with Lark and Margaret. Noel decides that he would like to live in

Vermont for good, and when a house near Charles and Sol comes on the market, he and the narrator buy it and move in. A few months later the narrator's former husband, David, and a girl named Patty come for a visit. "David seems not to feel awkward" about visiting his former wife, their child, and a former friend who is now living with his former wife. They all walk in the woods, chat, eat, and smoke pot together. When David and Patty leave, there *is* a brief awkwardness. No one knows quite what to say. "*Ciao,*" David says. "Thanks." "Yes," Patty says. "It was nice of you to do this." David backs the car down the steep driveway cautiously, "the way someone pulls a zipper after it's been caught. We wave, they disappear. That was easy." End of story.

The question inevitably intrudes: Why does anyone write in this or any other way about these people when one apparently has nothing of interest to say about them and they show no sign of being of interest? Why do readers want to read about them—in the hope that somehow eventually they will be revealed to be of interest? Unfortunately, Beattie's stories invite these questions again and again, and they fail to answer them. That is the chief reason they are so difficult to describe except in the mechanical form of plot summary—because there is so little in them of substance to describe. They are about situations and people who do not matter, and the little that Beattie does with and for them cannot make them matter.

It would come as a considerable relief to be able to say that in her novels Beattie has been able to overcome the deficiencies that are so obtrusive in most of her short stories. But unfortunately, one is honestly not able to say this. Her novels are actually short stories extended to book length, or more correctly, they are book-length *Beattie* short stories in the sense that they are crowded with descriptions of physical detail and concern the same sort of people who drift in and out of various quite ordinary situations without achieving either drama or revelation. In fact, they are very similar to Carver's characters in being essentially displaced persons who are separated from wives or lovers, out of work or unhappy at work, dysfunctional emotionally, moving morosely through life without zeal or direction. But they are mostly members of a younger generation than Carver's people, and they are not blue-collar losers. Instead, they are middle-class, usually college-educated, quite intelligent losers who, even if they are out of work, seem to have enough money to buy the necessities of survival and even some of the cheaper luxuries that are required to divert their attention from the meaninglessness of it all. They inhabit but do not really belong to the cluttered, sleazy contemporary urban environment of inexpensive Chinese and Mexican restaurants, dull small-time jobs, old cars that often do not start, unpaid bills, junk mail, and junk food.

In *Chilly Scenes of Winter*, for example, most of the central characters are young people in their twenties who are bored with their lives but do not have the impulse to try for anything better. One reason is that they share a common conviction that they have been betrayed by history, that everything better happened in the past, back in the sixties when they were in college and the youth movement gave them a sense of purpose and participation. Now in the seventies they feel like anachronisms left behind by the passage of time and conditioned to expect an excitement and fulfillment that somehow never came into being.

Charles, the protagonist of the novel, lives in an old house bequeathed him by his grandmother and works at a low-paying government job. His principal preoccupation is, as I have said, with his grief over the loss of Laura, the one girl he ever really cared for. His best friend, Sam, once wanted to go to law school but now sells jackets in a men's clothing store. He mourns the death of his dog. Charles's young sister, Susan, lives with a medical student at school but is visiting Charles for the Christmas holidays. Their mother is an alcoholic and deeply neurotic and often needs to be hospitalized. Her first husband, the father of Charles and Susan, is dead, and she is now married to a man named Pete whom Charles detests.

Much of the action, such as it is, takes place at Charles's house. Susan stays there during her visit, along with a girlfriend she has brought along from college. Sam is introduced to the girlfriend and in a few hours has taken her to bed. Sam later recuperates from pneumonia in the house and finally moves in with Charles, bringing with him a new dog. Charles manages to arrange a meeting with Laura, and by the end of the novel may or may not have persuaded her to become his lover once again.

All this is characteristically commonplace and emotionally benumbed. In order to be readable, it needs some element of dramatic intensity. But since the characters can scarcely generate sentience, let alone intensity, it has to be fed intravenously into the narrative in the form of extreme grotesqueness, which, luckily, the mother of Charles and Susan is there to provide.

When she first appears in the novel, she phones her children and says that she is in pain and plans to kill herself. They rush to her house and find her

> naked on the bed, her robe bunched in front of her. There is a heating pad, not turned on, dangling from the bed. . . . There are things all over the floor: *The Reader's Digest*, Pete's socks, cigarette packs, matches. . . . Their mother has stringy, dyed-red

> hair. . . . She wears purply-red lipstick even to bed. She had silicone implants before her marriage to Pete. She is sixty-one now, and has better breasts than Susan. Charles stares at her breasts. She is always naked. . . . In the bathroom there is another heating pad, plugged in and turned to "high." Susan pulls the plug out. There are movie magazines all over. . . . A cigarette is floating in the [bath] water. . . . There is a magazine at the bottom of the tub. Susan jerks her hand out.

The freewheeling anarchy of this scene comes as a welcome relief from the anomic atmosphere generated by Charles, Susan, and the other young people, although it serves little purpose beyond that except perhaps to suggest with not so very veiled self-righteousness just how snobbish the young feel toward the physical infirmities of the elderly and just how hard on the lives of their innocent children messy and undisciplined parents can be. On the other hand, the subtler message may be that however disturbing to the somnolence of their children, some parents at least are still able to feel and strike out against pain, and in the process exhibit a certain charmingly defiant eccentricity.

In any case, it should be said in fairness that here and there in the novel there are isolated passages that also have little to do with the advancement of the action but where Beattie displays a surprising talent for satire. Her treatment of a girl's flirtation with lesbianism while struggling to achieve total feminist liberation, the obsession of the younger generation with trendy clothes, ethnic food, and rock music—such passages are in themselves beautifully realized, and the prose throughout is first-rate, the documentation of details so thorough that one ends by knowing all there is to know about the external features of the characters. However, they are if anything drawn too literally from life, are seen too precisely as they would be seen in life if they were photographed by a ubiquitous camera, and of course the extreme verisimilitude of their portrayal causes them to be instantly recognizable as being the kind of quite ordinary people one has seen and known. But verisimilitude is not the equivalent of imaginative re-creation nor is recognition an acceptable substitute for insight, the special intuitive understanding that enables the genuine novelist to penetrate beneath the surfaces of his characters to the individualizing and invisible secrets of their thoughts and emotions. It would seem to be a truth with particular application to Beattie's fiction that if the unexamined life is not worth living, unexamined characters are finally not worth reading about.

▪ III ▪

Amy Hempel appears to be an even more extreme case than Beattie of chronic minimalist constipation. The few splintered fragments of prose that manage to get on her pages feel as though they have been parted with against the pressure of the greatest reluctance. Yet whatever has been withheld—if, in fact, anything has—does not remain suspended hauntingly in the background, as it does in Hemingway, to provide the illusion of hysteria suppressed or pain silently endured. Behind Hempel's prose there seems to be nothing but a chilly emotional void generated by either an incapacity to feel or a determination to express no feeling if one is there. What this signifies concerning Hempel's impulse to write in the first place, one can only ponder. But what she does condescend to write is offered with none of the customary orienting devices that serve in more conventional fiction to inform the reader about the setting of the action and the nature of the characters involved in it. Most of the time the reader does not know quite what is taking place or why or where and who the characters are, if indeed they are. They seem to be arbitrary and provisional constructs created for the purposes of bafflement or used to entice the reader into a false expectation that some significance is about to be revealed. But their existence is so uncertain that they might just as easily have said and done something else in some other place or they might have said and done nothing at all.

One representative sample of Hempel's work is a bit of prose called "Why I'm Here" included in her first collection, *Reasons to Live*, the contents of which of course do not provide any reasons. The narrator, who may or may not be a young girl, is taking a vocational-guidance test. Her counselor asks her to name a time when she is happy. In response the girl describes a way of life she presumably most enjoys. It involves a process of regularly moving from one apartment to another, during which she gets rid of nearly everything she owns and buys new things. "Move enough times," she says, "and you will never defrost a freezer." Her counselor then asks the girl, "What do you suppose would happen if you just stayed put? If you just stayed still long enough to think a thing through?" "I don't know," the girl replies. "I won't feel like myself." "Oh," says the counselor, "but you will—you are."

What all this is meant to signify is not easy to say. Is the girl intended to come through as cutely zany and impulsive, a wild, untameable spirit charming in her inability to "think a thing through"? Is Hempel offering herself as charming because she is unable to think this story through and, therefore, is continuing to feel like herself?

In "When It's Human Instead of When It's Dog," perhaps the best-known story in the collection, a cleaning lady named Mrs. Hatano arrives at the house of her employer whose wife has recently died. Coming in the front door Mrs. Hatano notices a stain on the hall carpet. She tries to remove it with a vinegar solution but is unsuccessful, so she calls Ruthie, another cleaning lady, for advice. Ruthie tells her that if the spot is dog urine, she might as well forget trying to remove it. However, Ruthie knows that in that house there are no dogs, and she has heard that on the day the man's wife died, he carried her down the stairs. The stain must have happened *then*. Mrs. Hatano later sprays the stain with carpet cleaner, which dries to a white powder. That evening after the man has had his dinner, Mrs. Hatano notices that he sees the stain. "The white-traced shape," which at first looked like "a state on a map" looks now "like a chalk-drawn victim on a sidewalk." When Mrs. Hatano leaves the house, she takes her wages of forty dollars from the table in the hall but leaves a five-dollar bill "because she could not get the spot out."

This quasi-epiphany may be intended to tell us that from a cleaning lady's point of view what is important is that she could not remove the stain. Whether it was made by dog or human urine makes no difference so far as she is concerned. Mrs. Hatano is thus revealed to be cruelly without pity for the grieving man, or is she being simply professional as well as singularly obtuse? Like the dogs in Auden's "Musée des Beaux Arts" is she merely going on with her doggy life untouched by the fact that a tragic event has lately occurred in the house? It is impossible to say because Hempel offers us too little evidence for interpretation. The man's grief is never characterized or explicitly revealed and neither is Mrs. Hatano.

▪ IV ▪

In my first critical book, *After the Lost Generation*, published in 1951, I tried to define the nature of the influence *The New Yorker* magazine seemed at the time to exert over the newer American fiction writers who were beginning to appear in the first years after World War II. Although the discussion had to do with the work of an altogether different group of writers, its application to the fiction now being produced by Ann Beattie, Amy Hempel, and particularly Frederick Barthelme, whose stories have appeared almost exclusively in *The New Yorker*, seems to me to be uncannily close.

"The writing that comes out of this [*The New Yorker*] world," I wrote, "is distinguished by its overwhelming accuracy, its painful attention to detail. Produced out of a morbid fear of emotion, it loses itself in trivia so that it will not have to express emotion. It derives its power from a skillful arrangement of the endless unimportances which make up its parts—scraps of brittle dialogue, bits of carefully contrived scene and setting, little stifled orgasms of dramatic climax. But more than anything else, it is assured writing, rich with the wisdom of sour experience in the countless minor bars of many continents. Never is there a mischosen word, an inept phrase, a misplaced emphasis. It all has the slick perfection of freshly laid concrete, as if it had all been produced at the same moment by the same machine."

I went on to offer evidence for these generalizations in an analysis of Irwin Shaw's *The Young Lions*, a war novel I saw as the perfect embodiment of the worst features of *The New Yorker* influence. But with some very minor modifications they apply equally well to the fiction of Beattie, Hempel, and Barthelme, although if anything the features I described have over the years become visibly more exaggerated in their work. There is even more preoccupation than there was before with surface detail and trivia. The prose is even more polished and assured, but there is no longer evidence that it has been "enriched by the wisdom of sour experience" in bars or anywhere else. Those "bits of carefully contrived scene and setting" survive but in still smaller bits, while the "little stifled orgasms of dramatic climax" have disappeared altogether. What is left in the fiction of these writers is a kind of narcissistic literary language that seems to be mostly infatuated with its own stylistic felicities and that offers only tiny, extremely reluctant glimpses of experiences that are so lacking in vitality they cannot be brought to even stifled orgasm.

Like his brother Donald, Frederick Barthelme has for years been a regular writer for *The New Yorker*, and even though the two men show in their fiction little family resemblance to each other, they both might have been created for the sole and specific purpose of becoming *New Yorker* writers. Each commands a prose style that in its combination of high polish and low dramatic voltage is especially attractive to the magazine's clientele. But they use language to serve quite different ends. Donald is a much more radical experimentalist than Frederick, and his short stories in particular are evidently intended to project a wildly hallucinatory vision of the trivialization of contemporary life, an effect they usually achieve through an excessive accumulation of the details of trivia as well as fragmented scenes and wraithlike people. I once observed that, in fact, Donald's stories are quite literally verbal immersions in dreck, the evacuated crud and muck of the contemporary world, and they very effectively create the sensations of being suffocated and shat upon and generally soiled and despoiled in soul and mind that accompany much of our daily experience of that world.

Actually, both brothers write almost exclusively about

trivia. But where there is a satirical edge to Donald's treatment of it, which helps to preserve him from succumbing to the fallacy of imitative form, Frederick writes about trivia seemingly without in the least recognizing it as such. The environment of his fiction is one of trendy designer decor and fashionable brand names, about which he is nearly as knowledgeable as Tom Wolfe. But unlike Wolfe, he offers them straight, as if with honest admiration. For example, he can be downright loving in his enumeration of the furnishings of such a prosaic structure as a business office. In the opening paragraph of the story called "Box Step" he introduces a young woman named Ann who we quickly realize is herself actually part of the office decor and is destined to remain so throughout the remainder of the story. Ann is "pretty, divorced, a product model who didn't go far because of her skin, which is very fair and freckled." The two floors of the office have recently been done in "charcoal carpet, ribbed wallcovering, chipboard-gray upholstery, and gunmetal Levolors; the windows were already tinted." There is no hint of irony here or in any of the other copious descriptions of physical detail to be found in Frederick's stories. They are not used to expose his characters as pretentious or fatuous, and they do nothing to advance the action. In fact, they often constitute virtually all the action that there is, which is to say that like his brother, Frederick seems unable to create dramatic movement or involvement or an ultimate dramatic revelation in his stories. Indeed, it is almost as if both men consciously avoid such effects and view them with a kind of fastidious horror as representing some final vulgarity of taste, some shameful breach of fictional decorum. Again and again Frederick in particular will assemble people and places, bring them into brief relation with one another, and then stop short of letting anything result from the encounter.

The typical situation in Frederick's fiction involves a

meeting between the youngish male narrator-protagonist and some woman. It is uncertain whether they actually feel attracted to each other, but since they happen to be in the same place at the same time, they may converse, share a meal, and even spend a night or two in bed together. Then, although nothing specifically goes wrong, they drift apart as if the emotional risk of further intimacy—if that it can be called—were too high or some failure of energy made it seem not worthwhile.

The male narrator serves as a conduit through which the factual materials of the story are presented. But he gives them no emphasis or coloration. He is resolutely atonal and displays neither humor nor irony in response to the experiences he records. He appears in some stories to be not only affectless but infantile. In "Box Step" he occupies but is never shown to work in the trendily decorated office where for his diversion he keeps ant farms and an electronic baseball game. Throughout the story he displays something like interest only in a toy rubber dinosaur. In "Shopgirls" he is a watcher of attractive women who work in a department store. It turns out that three of them have for some time been aware of his attention, and they invite him to lunch, ostensibly to decide which of them will ask him to come home with her. The girl named Andrea is selected and takes him to her apartment. There she prepares dinner; they eat; and he beds down for the night, fully clothed, on the sofa. "When she decides to go to bed you make no move to follow her into the bedroom, and she makes no special invitation." Later he imagines that "on a sunny day in the middle of the week" he drives to the mall in a new car and buys "a wood-handled spatula from a lovely girl with clean short hair." End of story.

In "Monster Deal," under the name of Jerry Bergen, he rents a house from a man named Elliot who is out of the country for a year. A young woman named Tina arrives at the door and tells Bergen that she is accustomed to staying with Elliot whenever she is in town and that they have a regular arrangement that when she stays, she is to buy the dinner. Bergen agrees to let her stay. It happens that he has made a date with Karen, the girl who delivers his newspaper. When she arrives that afternoon, Tina displays a strong interest in Karen's Jeepster and then decides to accompany her on her paper route. She and Karen leave carrying a bottle of bourbon and glasses, and they do not return until the next morning. Obviously drunk, Karen tells Bergen that they have spent the night in the woods. Then she and Tina go to bed together. Later that day Tina leaves while Karen is still asleep, and Bergen eats a meal and starts to read the newspaper. "But then," he says at the story's end, "I don't want to read, I just want to look at the headlines."

At no point in the narrative are we given the faintest clue as to Bergen's attitude toward what is happening, whatever that may be. He is so aloof throughout that he might as well not be present. He attaches no significance to the entry of Tina into his life, and he sees none in her sudden and bizarre attraction to Karen. It all simply happens, and that is all.

One cannot help but wonder what there is about such stories that makes them appealing, particularly to the supposedly sophisticated readers of *The New Yorker*. Do these readers find comfort in a fiction in which nothing of significance happens, in which encounters between people come to nothing, and life goes on in a curiously somnambulistic way for the characters? Would genuine fictional climax and revelation be somehow disturbing to them? One can theorize that perhaps for them the stories not only of the Barthelmes but of Beattie and Hempel represent a kind of literary tranquilizer that can be ingested without harmful side effects and that provides the highly temporary relief of mild sedation at a somewhat more exalted level than that provided by television. Also, since they do offer a set of characters and the materials of an at least potentially dramatic situation, they undoubtedly generate in the reader pleasurable feelings of anticipation that something is about to happen. But when the characters fail to develop and the drama does not materialize, he can perhaps find confirmation for what he knew all along: that life is an enigma or simply meaningless, that nothing ever *really* happens, and he might as well not bother his head any further about it. If this is in fact the case, then one can only observe that as a statement about the nature of existence, this may have a degree of plausibility but is extremely superficial and provides no insight whatever into the kind of truth that the writer, through the very act of placing his work on public view, puts himself under some real obligation to explore.

▪ CHAPTER III ▪

MEDIUM WITHOUT MESSAGE

▪

The writers I have so far discussed are most notable for having produced a fiction in which technique is paramount and content is as negligible as it is lacking in thematic point. It is a kind of fiction that resembles very closely the still life in painting and those mechanical exercises pianists perform to improve their digital dexterity. What is important in both cases is the manner in which the performance is executed and not what the performance depicts or interprets. The bowl of fruit on the velvet-covered table in the still life could just as easily be an Egyptian vase or a bust of Beethoven, while for the exercising pianist melody is abandoned in favor of the speed and grace with which his fingers move across the keyboard.

It is of interest that certain music critics have recently observed that younger pianists who perform in prize contests have become increasingly similar to one another in their degree of technical competence but seem equally unable to offer original and dynamic interpretations of the works they perform. As one critic remarked, nobody faints at their performances. And, surely, nobody faints at the performances of Carver, Beattie, Hempel, Mason, and the others.

What appears to have happened, among both younger pianists and writers, is that through much the same evolutionary process that has enabled science to apply its techniques with increasing efficiency to the mass production of commodity goods, it has become possible steadily to improve technical efficiency in the mass production of creative writing, piano recitals, and other forms of commodity culture.

Partly because of the influence of the graduate schools, we have been able virtually to abolish plain bad writing from the formerly egalitarian precincts of literature. Gone are those clumsily composed, implausibly plotted novels that used to be a common feature of the early work of aspiring writers, and that in the case of tone-deaf duffers like Lewis, Dreiser, and Farrell became a lifelong feature. Today it seems to be taken for granted that, whatever else may be wrong with a novel, it will of course be well written, even if one finds it extremely difficult to distinguish its prose from that of a hundred others.

But unfortunately, we have not witnessed a comparable evolution in the range, depth, or sophistication of the subject matter treated through the medium of that impeccable prose—a fact that may seem surprising unless one adheres to the quite plausible view that the achievement of a uniform competence in the writing of prose must necessarily be accompanied by a uniform sameness in the conception of subject matter. And this, in turn, would seem to imply that there is a sameness of both sensibility and experience among the writers who are doing the conceiving.

In fact, if one examines the work of some of the younger writers who appear to be very different in their approach to fiction from Carver, Beattie, and the others, one finds considerable evidence that this may indeed be the case. The writers I have in mind cannot by any of the usual definitions of the term be called minimalists, for they tend to produce a fiction that is very often quite conventionally realistic and that contains reasonably lifelike characters occupying a much more fully created dramatic milieu. In short, they appear to represent, at least in style, the very opposite of minimalism. Yet they frequently share with the minimalists a common deficiency, for even though they may encompass far larger quantities of experience with a far greater realism, they fail, as a rule, to endow that experience with sufficient thematic significance to justify their extensive treatment of it. Their work typically makes little or no specific social, political, or critical comment on the material it concerns, but seems designed to produce a wholly uninflected landscape-painting effect of verisimilitude, a mirror image of reality that is offered simply for its own sake.

William Kennedy, who is in many ways the best of the newer realists, can, for example, write brilliantly in his cycle of Albany novels about the dreary lives of the down-and-out: street people drunk, cold, and hungry, drifting in rags from one makeshift shelter to another. Yet behind these portraits of profound human misery there is no evident reformist zeal, no anger at the social system in part responsible for them, and no suggestion that the portraits are intended to exemplify something larger than themselves—in the sense that Joyce's Bloom becomes a figure symbolic of the modern urban citizen and his Dublin a microcosm of the modern city, or that Jay Gatsby takes on the dimension of American romantic idealism doomed to be destroyed in circumstances that are inhumanely materialistic. Kennedy's people are presented as and for what they are, without implicit thematic emphasis or coloration.

Anne Tyler's much admired novel, *Breathing Lessons*, may well be much admired because it is lightly entertaining and guaranteed to be offensive to no one. It is a straightforward, realistic account of a car trip taken by a middle-aged woman and her husband to attend the wedding of an old friend. During the course of the journey the woman is gradually revealed to be a well-meaning but inept manipulator of family events and relationships so that they will conform to her idealized vision of things. She is, in short, a most promising subject for satire or even, one might dare to suppose, a fairly devastating dissection of a certain type of motherly woman who, in her desire for control over other people's lives, is something of a monster. But Tyler's characterization of her is so mild and good-natured, so carefully nonjudgmental, that it finally has no thrust or bite. The novel, in fact, is much too wholesome for its own good, too kindly a mirror held up to nature. The image it reflects, while perfectly recognizable, is scarcely illuminating, for if, as Percy Lubbock said, "the best form [in fiction] is that which makes the most of its subject," then *Breathing Lessons* represents a failure of form. It does not make the most of its subject, which is potentially a study of malevolence operating under the guise of good will, because Tyler clearly was so blinded by her own good will that she could not recognize what her subject was.

■ II ■

On first reading, the fiction of Bobbie Ann Mason strikes one as being a refreshing departure from the extreme and essentially arid minimalism practiced in their different ways by Beattie, Hempel, and the Barthelmes. Mason seems, first of all, to have embraced without apology most of the conventions of old-style fiction, and she employs them with a good deal of energy and skill, as if she had always felt at home in them and never needed to consider the possibility of writing in some other more fashionable way. Perhaps because she is what used to be called a local colorist and writes almost always about the southern experience, one encounters in her work such traditional fictive materials as genuine social environment, characters who take on substance through the complex interacting relationship that is created when people actually inhabit an environment, share membership in a family, community, and region, and know in their bones that they have some real connection with a past that extends farther back in time than last Saturday night.

Mason is also astonishingly well informed about the environment she writes about, and her large fund of information on such subjects as popular culture and provincial values enables her to name and dramatize factual details so as to enrich the realism of her narrative and not become merely a diversionary substitute for it. Her abiding interest is in the lives led by southerners who belong to the blue collar and lower middle classes and whose happy preoccupation with the sleaze and trivia of their milieu is their equivalent of the unhappy upper-middle-class preoccupation with a rather more expensive kind of sleaze and trivia to be found in the fiction of Beattie, Hempel, and the Barthelmes. Mason's people—and they are mostly women—are the sort who work at insecure, low-paying jobs as waitresses at McDonald's or clerks in department stores, who work because they have to, bear children because they get pregnant rather than because they want to, feel disappointment and frustration without knowing why, and are generally helpless to help themselves. Their modest pleasures consist of buying cut-rate clothes and makeup, visiting shopping malls and fast-food restaurants, and taking trips by camper to Disneyland, Sea World, and Opryland. Few of them have traveled far outside Kentucky, and those who have, particularly those who have been to Detroit or Chicago, are looked upon with some awe and envy. To read about these people is to recognize them instantly, and Mason brings them vividly to life as exemplary figures of their class and region.

But what she somehow does not bring to life is their

significance, the manner in which their experience tells us something fundamental about the human condition, and as I have indicated, this is a failing she shares with a large number of her contemporaries who employ prose techniques very different from hers. But in her case it is obviously not an excessive minimalism that stands in the way of revelation, nor is it some fastidiousness about drawing inferences from the experience she so realistically records. Rather, it appears to reside in a certain inability on her part to extricate herself sufficiently from the very documentary realism that gives her work its authenticity to find in it thematic justification for the effort she has made to assemble all the realistic details. This is to say that her fiction, particularly her stories, consists of a series of extremely well written and closely observed non sequiturs—not in the sense that they do not logically follow but in the sense that little or nothing thematically meaningful follows from them.

In a story called "Offerings," included in Mason's first collection, *Shiloh and Other Stories*, the assemblage of details is intricate and impressively evocative of the manners and values of southern working-class life. A woman named Sandra, who is separated from her husband, is visited by her mother and grandmother at the rundown farm where she is living. She serves them dinner and afterwards they watch a movie on television. Then Sandra and her mother go out to bring in the ducks from the pond so that the foxes will not kill them during the night. Outside, the mother smokes a cigarette, which she cannot do in front of the grandmother. While standing at the edge of the pond, Sandra recalls hearing during the previous week the cry of a wildcat, and she thinks that she would not mind if the wildcat took her ducks. "They are her offering." That is effectively the end of the story, and it sounds portentous. But what it portends is not easy to say because so little evidence is given of Sandra's mood and situation that one does not know to whom or what the offering is made or what an offering signifies to her. The problem is that, as so often happens in Mason's stories, the social milieu is closely described but the message is obscure, perhaps because obscured by the very closeness of the description.

In another of her stories called "Midnight Magic" from the later collection, *Love Life*, the central character, a young man named Steve, drives a garishly decorated car with "Midnight Magic" painted on its rear. Steve's girlfriend, Karen, attends Sunday night meetings presided over by Sardo, a mystic alleged to be a thousand-year-old American Indian inhabiting the body of a teenage girl who drives a Porsche. After a night of drinking with Karen, during which they quarrel, Steve takes his dirty clothes to a laundromat and cleans up his apartment in the hope that he can persuade Karen to move in with him. But when he asks her to do so, her response is ambiguous, even though she has been frightened by reports of a rapist in the area where she lives and sleeps with a shotgun under her bed. She tells Steve that she has letters to write and needs to "get her head together" in preparation for the evening's meeting with Sardo.

While driving to the airport to pick up friends of his who have just been married, Steve sees what appears to be a dead man lying beside the highway. The story ends when he stops at a phone booth and reports the sighting to the police.

The problem here is that the elements brought together—"Midnight Magic," Sardo, the rapist, the dead man—are not dramatically related to one another and, therefore, do nothing to develop a thematic statement. Steve is a not very bright young man adrift in a banal existence, and he may be meant to be a caricature of American car fetishism. Karen may be meant to be a caricature of the current spiritualism craze. But both are so thinly characterized that they remain enigmas. All the narrative details project an effect of oddity and dislocation, and they do come together to form a vivid, if somewhat askew impression of life. But it is not an *interpretation* of life, for it is not comprehended by a guiding principle, a governing thematic intention.

Nearly all Mason's stories are like this—beautifully composed impressions of life—and nearly all suffer from this same failure to interpret. Interestingly enough, it is in her first novel, *In Country*, rather than in her stories that Mason is able to achieve genuine significance. There the young girl's effort to reproduce in her own life the Vietnam war experiences of her dead father is freshly imagined and completely convincing. *In Country* is, in fact, a finely written and thematically successful novel, and it may well be an indication that the novel is the form she might do well to explore more extensively in the future.

▪ III ▪

In his otherwise negative assessment of the newer short story writers Madison Bell makes an exception of Mary Robison, saying that at least in her stories the characters are allowed freedom: "Instead of being shoved around by technique like checkers on a board, they seem to speak and act for themselves." While one can understand how Bell might have arrived at this impression, one wonders whether he has interpreted the evidence quite correctly. It could be argued that if Robison's characters seem free, it is because they are undisciplined by any controlling authorial intention, and so are at liberty to wander at will into the narrative and do there whatever they like, often to the surprise of the reader and, one might even suppose, to Robison herself. I have said that Mason's fiction shows evidence of being similarly uncontrolled, but the effect is very different. Mason's problem seems to be that her excessive preoccupation with physical detail obscures, if not altogether nullifies, any possibility of clear-cut thematic statement. For Robison the nullifying preoccupation is not so much with detail as with an almost narcissistic relationship she maintains with her characters, whom she appears to find irresistibly lovable. For example, in her extremely entertaining first novel, entitled simply *O!*, the charmingly eccentric and seemingly quite pointless behavior of the characters appears to be the sole subject. They are cute and adorable members of the same family who spend their days lounging around their large and elegant house and exchanging a great deal of smarty dialogue. They bear a close resemblance to Salinger's Glass family both in the sense that they are nearly as adorable and because the justification for their story seems to be that just being in their presence and hearing them talk is such a rare and delightful privilege that nothing more needs to be offered. And in fact throughout most of the narrative nothing is—no motivation for their behavior, no background information to speak of, no examination of their personalities. It is only at the end that one learns that much about them may possibly be explained by the fact that the mother, who disappeared when the brother and sister were quite young, turns out not to have migrated to Ireland as they had always supposed but had become mentally unbalanced and been confined to a sanitarium where she died. This revelation shocks and dismays her children, who had planned to visit their mother in Ireland, and causes them to indulge in some hysterical and self-destructive but still charming behavior as they struggle to adjust to this new version of their family history. Their resemblance to the Glass family is indeed close. But they possess no equivalent of Franny's compensatory mysticism, Zooey's sentimental effort to help her, or the trauma of Seymour's suicide. Nothing, in fact, occurs in the action to give point to their characters or meaning to their behavior until the sad news about the mother is revealed. But by then it is too late. The novel becomes, therefore, a chronicle of attractively zany but unmotivated behavior brought to a climax by the introduction of an overly melodramatic deus ex machina.

Here and in most of her short stories Robison shows evidence of sharing in the deficiency that appears monotonously to afflict so many of the writers previously discussed: She is unable to make a sufficient virtue out of not knowing what she means. It may be, however, that since so much of her fiction first appeared in *The New Yorker*, that deficiency has been recognized, at least by the magazine, to be itself a virtue. Nevertheless, in story after story characters and setting are presented, and nothing of significance results.

In the title story of her collection *An Amateur's Guide to the Night*, one finds the familiar Robison scenario—attractively eccentric characters, clever dialogue, certain narrative clues that slyly hint at eventual revelation. There are a seventeen-year-old girl who is addicted to studying the stars through her telescope; her thirty-five-year-old mother who looks young enough to be able to introduce herself as her daughter's sister when they double-date; and a grandfather who shares a house with them. The mother is more than slightly dotty, believes she has a brain tumor, and talks of her "light pills," which she says give her a "recharge" so that she does not need very much sleep. She also apparently checks herself into a hospital from time to time, although it is uncertain whether this is true or another one of her fantasies. She, the daughter, and the grandfather spend their evenings watching television horror films with titles like *The Creeper* and *White Zombie*.

There are a few small happenings in the story that might be considered potential dramatic events: the daughter's high school graduation, which the mother may or may not have attended, and a bus trip they take together to go shopping in Terre Haute. During the trip they pass the hospital where the mother may or may not stay from time to time, and the mother sees on the bus a man she believes is a plainclothes police officer who is trailing them. At the end of the story the daughter receives a card from her absent father congratulating her on her graduation. She thinks that if her father, who is now remarried, ever returned, he would have a hard time understanding them and the way they do things. "He would have to do some thinking." This is undoubtedly true, for they certainly are an odd group of people. But it is also true that Robison should have done a great deal more thinking before she wrote the story, because it is an assemblage of details that might have come to signify but in their present unexamined condition clearly do not.

Another story in the collection, "The Dictionary in the Laundry Chute," is perhaps a somewhat different case, for at least one can guess at a possible interpretation. A middle-aged couple are nursing their grown daughter who has had a mental breakdown, is an alcoholic, and does not eat or sleep regularly. The story's title is taken from a brief scene in which the girl's father drops a dictionary down a laundry chute to dislodge some piece of clothing stuck there. It is a practical measure taken to perform a practical function, and it is possible that it is meant to be associated with the father's concluding statement to his wife. "So we treat her [the daughter] with kid gloves for a while. We keep her away from the drinking. Make sure she takes those pills. . . . Feed her like a calf for the fair. That's all we got to do. Isn't it?" "Yes," the mother replies.

These also are practical measures to be taken to achieve a practical end. But of course they do not begin to address the seriousness and complexity of the daughter's condition.

Hence, the apparent irony of the closing lines: "Well, then I don't get it," the father says. "Honest, I don't get it. I mean. I don't see why we aren't happier and why we can't *all* get a little sleep around here." This may be a plausible reading of the story except for one detail. There is no earned connection between the practical solution to the problem with the laundry chute and the practical measures that need to be taken to help the daughter. If the father had been developed fully as a person who thinks that all problems have a practical solution, then the story might have become a poignant commentary on the grave limitations of that point of view. But as it stands, the father and the story as a whole are too thinly drawn to support such an interpretation.

In reading Robison's fiction one feels rather like the woman in "Your Errant Mom," another of her stories, who overhears but can make no sense of fragments of conversation between two people sitting in the seat ahead of her on a train. Robison's tendency throughout her work is to be coyly, even cutely enigmatic, and she is so much in love with her characters that she evidently feels no need to make them either lovable or understandable to her readers. If Madison Bell congratulates her on allowing her characters freedom, one might suggest that she would be better off if she allowed them a good deal less and required them to become subservient to some thematic idea that they should exist to serve.

▪ IV ▪

Louise Erdrich in her novel *The Beet Queen* is a somewhat different case and one that deserves close attention. Like its predecessor, *Love Medicine*, the novel is written, for the most part, in the form of a family saga that centers on the lives of three siblings, their relatives, and friends. All the characters are presented polyphonically, as a series of voices describing the action from their individual points of view over a period of forty years, from 1932 to 1972.

The story begins when the three siblings, Mary and Karl Adare and their infant brother, are abandoned by their mother in a moment of freakish impulse when she buys a ticket for a church fair airplane ride and simply flies away with the pilot, who later becomes her husband. The infant brother is taken by a man named Miller who gives the child to his wife as a replacement for the baby she has lost. The little boy adopts the name of Jude Miller and grows up to become a priest.

Mary and Karl, who are eleven and fourteen respectively, make their way by boxcar to Argus, North Dakota, where they hope to be given a home by their mother's sister, Fritzie, who, with her husband, Pete, runs a butcher shop in the town. But moments after they arrive, Karl is frightened by a barking dog, climbs back into the boxcar, and there has a homosexual encounter with a hobo, after which he leaps off the train, is injured, and is cared for by an Indian woman named Fleur Pillager, an enormous creature who makes a living as an itinerant peddler.

In the meantime, Mary has found her aunt and settled down to live with her and her husband and her beautiful young cousin, Sita, whom Mary comes to despise, partly for her narcissism, partly because she becomes a rival for the attentions of Mary's best friend, a tall, muscular Chippewa woman named Celestine James.

Obviously, there is potential here for high melodrama with the narrative canvas almost as heavily populated with strange characters and bizarre events as a novel by Dickens or Balzac. The problem of course is how to make it all *mean* something, and in her effort to find a solution Erdrich came up with the idea of providing her characters with certain traumatic or otherwise critical experiences that would bring forth epiphanies of insight and prove to have a major influence in determining their behavior throughout the remainder of the novel. Thus, Mary is conditioned to become a mystic and compulsive palm-reading teller of fortunes when as a child she plunges headfirst down an ice-covered slide at school and produces on impact a pattern in the ice in which the Catholic sisters see the face of Christ and proclaim it a miracle. Karl is devastated by his mother's desertion of the family, seeks love from the hobo in the boxcar, and by the time he reaches adulthood has become firmly established as a practicing homosexual. The beautiful Sita becomes obsessed with visions of wealth and the glamorous life, works briefly as a department store fashion model, after which she contrives to open a high-gourmet restaurant in Argus. When that fails, she suffers a breakdown and slides into insanity.

Wallace Pfef, a friend of Celestine and Mary and the developer of the beet industry in Argus, has what is evidently the one homosexual relationship of his life with Karl at a sales convention and is forever haunted by the memory. Dot, Celestine's daughter by, of all people, Karl, appears to have been born hateful, and she frightens and alienates her classmates at school, is humiliated when a fellow cast member in a Christmas play behaves boorishly, and is further humiliated when Mary gets drunk and ruins the birthday party Wallace has arranged for her. She is, therefore, made permanently angry and resentful, at least until just before the end of the novel.

If it were not for the excellence of the prose, there would be very little in this narrative to distinguish it from the kinds of novels that are to be found at airport newsstands and that one reads to avoid noticing that one is in the air. But as is often the case with such novels, there are certain inconsistencies here that require one to suspend a considerable amount of disbelief. For example, Karl fathers Dot by

Celestine after encountering her for the first time when he arrives in Argus ostensibly to see his sister, Mary. He has been absent for so many years that when he sees Celestine, he assumes she is Mary, and after the mistake is corrected, he is immediately overcome by a fierce passion for her. Although she is a wholly unattractive woman, it may be her mannish muscularity that he finds irresistible. In any case, she finds nothing irresistible about him. Yet in a very few minutes they fall in a tangle of fevered limbs to the floor where they proceed vigorously to copulate. It is the first time that Celestine has had sex; in fact, all she knows about male-female love is what she has read in cheap romantic novels. But the problem there is that the love scenes always stopped just short of sex, so it is forever unclear whether Karl's performances on the floor and later in bed come up to her innocent expectations. But then it is unclear until the end of the novel whether she feels very much about anything.

There are other unsolved mysteries such as exactly why Sita goes insane, whether Dot is nothing more than the surly sum of the persecutions she believes she has suffered, of course through no fault of her own, at the hands of other people, and why Wallace and Celestine continue to put up with her when she is so unlovable and treats them so badly. In addition, both Mary and Karl remain enigmatic throughout, and Karl floats in and out of the action seemingly without purpose, while Celestine's brother, Russell, the "most decorated" war veteran, appears to function solely as a figure of inscrutable oddity and perhaps to provide a bit of local color.

Nevertheless, in the climactic final scene of the novel all requirements of mere logic are sacrificed in a rollicking orchestration of bizarreness that nearly causes one to forget that such requirements ever existed.

On the day of the Beet Parade and the crowning of the

Beet Queen, Mary and Celestine arrive at Sita's house to take her into town for the parade. They find her standing, all in white, in some yew bushes at the front of the house. She is staring at them through the dry needles and looks impatient. But when they approach closer, they discover that Sita is dead and is standing because her necklace has been snagged on a broken branch and is holding up her head.

Because they do not know what else to do and are afraid to leave Sita alone, the two women carry her to Mary's truck and manage to maneuver her into the front seat, where she sits, "her hands in her lap, her head slightly cocked, gazing out the front windshield." Then they drive into town, park behind the grandstand, and leave Sita sitting in the truck and looking as though she were alive, her expression one of deep watchfulness.

Meanwhile, Russell, who is now confined to a wheelchair after suffering a stroke, is dressed in his Army uniform and medals and is hoisted onto a parade float decorated to resemble a field of graves, each covered with plastic grass and red poppies. A white cross is planted at his feet. As the procession moves down the street, Russell falls asleep and dreams that he is dead. " 'He looks stuffed,' cried a shrill woman from the curb."

While all this is going on and by truly remarkable coincidence, the young brother of Karl and Mary, now a priest named Father Miller, arrives in Argus in long-delayed response to a letter from Sita telling his foster mother about his true identity and the location of Sita's family in Argus. Father Miller finds the butcher shop, but since it is deserted, he joins the crowd of townspeople moving toward the parade.

Then it turns out that by another coincidence no less remarkable, Karl also arrives in Argus and proceeds to the fairgrounds where he sees Mary's parked truck with the dead Sita sitting in the front seat. He gets into the truck beside her, speaks to her without realizing she is dead, and briefly falls asleep. He awakens just in time to see his old lover, Wallace, sitting on a stool suspended above a dunk tank. Dot appears, obviously in a rage, buys three softballs that are used to dunk the stool-sitter if thrown accurately, and with her first throw she drops Wallace into the tank. Karl runs to the tank, falls into it, and pulls Wallace out.

In the final pages of the novel most of the principal characters—Celestine, Mary, Father Miller, who of course does not recognize his sister and is never seen again, and Karl and Wallace, both dripping wet—are seated in the grandstand, and we learn what it was that provoked Dot's savage attack on Wallace. It seems that he has rigged the election of the Beet Queen so that Dot will win and finally, finally have something nice happen to her. It is when Dot hears of this that she makes her attack, and afterwards she decides to do what her grandmother and her father had done—escape by flight. She accordingly runs from the platform where she is about to be crowned Beet Queen and climbs into an airplane that is supposed to write her name in smoke in the sky and at the same time seed the clouds with silver-iodide for rain.

When the airplane lands, Dot sees that the grandstand is empty, that evidently no one has cared enough to wait to make sure she came down safely. But then she notices her mother sitting alone, waiting for her. At that moment and in complete contradiction of everything we have come to know about her, Dot senses in Celestine's eyes "the force of her love." They return home, Celestine prepares toast and eggs, Dot goes up to her room alone. But now, magically transformed by her recognition of her mother's love, she thinks tenderly of her "lying in the next room, her covers thrown back . . . eyes wide open, waiting." And with that the novel ends.

This final scene is rendered with great skill and is in its way quite moving. But the emotion is earned at the expense of a sudden and highly implausible rehabilitation of Dot's character, and surely that is not all the novel is supposed to be about. It is much more likely that Erdrich intended to say something of larger significance about the various ways in which certain tensions, mistakes, failures of nerve, and misunderstandings can destroy the relations of people who are bound together, however tenuously, by the ties of blood. If so, her intention was altogether honorable and might have resulted in a novel of some real depth and resonance. But to serve such a theme effectively, the novel would have had to be presented as a chronicle of character development and revelation that, ideally, would dramatize the complex ramifications of the emotional conflicts underlying the action. In fact, there is evidence to indicate that Erdrich may have hoped that her narrative would become a chronicle of just this kind. How else is one to account for the presence of such a large cast of characters, most of whom are related to one another, and who are examined and self-examined in such close detail over a period of forty years? Yet the problem is that the characters do not develop, unless Dot's dubious epiphany at the end can be said to represent development. Instead, each of their identities is created early on and seemingly fixed forever in a single, usually stunted relation to reality as the result of one or more of the aforementioned traumatic and/or apocalyptic events that occur at some vulnerable moment in their lives.

This method of creating identity might be acceptable in a novel by Zola or a naturalistic throwback like Farrell. But philosophically it represents a rationale that has been untenable for at least the last one hundred years. It assumes a mechanical universe governed by immutable law and force and a static view of human character as simply a chemical and ganglionic response to environmental stimuli; and that is not the universe we have inhabited or a view we have been able sensibly to hold since the appearance of Freud and the publication, in 1905, of the first Einstein papers.

Its presence in a work by a presumably sophisticated late-twentieth-century writer like Erdrich is, therefore, anachronistic and serves to impoverish her vision of her characters by depriving them of free will and reducing them to synthetic figures who cannot be brought to dramatic life because they have no capacity for growth or change. It is a rationale that makes it possible for Erdrich to imply that Sita, in the absence of other discernible causes, goes insane, as does the mother of Mary, Karl, and Father Miller, simply because they are linked by bad genes. But genetic inheritance cannot be considered, at least since Ibsen, to be a firm basis for characterization. It is biology. And to say that someone is mentally or emotionally unstable has no meaning in fiction unless the instability is shown to have some dramatic purpose, some vital relation to the developing action. At least when Lady Macbeth goes insane, we are made fully aware of the powerful reasons for it, just as we are made aware of its powerful consequences. When Sita goes insane, it remains merely an effect of unjustified grotesquerie.

What we have, then, is an extremely well written novel that is flawed by an outmoded and grossly limited conception of human character and in which far too much of the dramatic interest is generated by bizarre or inexplicable events such as Sita's insanity and the macabre treatment of her corpse, the miraculous appearance of Christ's face in the shattered ice after Mary's plunge down the schoolyard slide, the introduction of Father Miller into a scene in which he takes no part, the cutely contrived coincidence whereby Dot and her grandmother both fly away in an airplane, and the wholly gratuitous presence of Russell in uniform and medals atop the parade float. All the characters, in fact, are notable chiefly for their eccentricities, and the reason may be that they are essentially flat characters who need to be presented as peculiar if they are to be interesting at all.

This kind of easy evasion of the difficult task of creating characters in full complexity and depth is a feature of the work of more than a few of the new minimalists and many of their realist contemporaries. Like them, Erdrich seems to possess abundant raw materials for fiction. But she evidently lacks the ability to take complete imaginative possession of those materials and employ them in the service of a significantly developed dramatic theme. Her novel might be described in Aristotelian terms as consisting primarily of "spectacle," and however strange, violent, or perverse the spectacle may be, it is only one element, and a minor one, in a drama of which the central concern is or should be with characters confronting a fateful moment of crisis in their relation to themselves and to their society, a crisis dramatized with such power and endowed with such meaning that at the end of it neither they nor we are ever again quite as we were.

■ CHAPTER IV ■

ANGUISH AS A SECOND LANGUAGE

■

If Erdrich's intended but largely unrealized theme in the novel is the breakdown of family relationships, David Leavitt deals more directly and, on the whole, more successfully with the effects of that breakdown on the lives of the children of divorce, rejected spouses, and other casualties of the war between the sexes. Given such a subject, it is not surprising that Leavitt's fiction is burdened by a heavy weight of anxiety over the fragility of human connections, the difficulty of achieving and sustaining love, the collapse of the once stabilizing structures of loyalty and responsibility, and, above all, the perpetual threat of physical and emotional death.

Of the nine stories included in *Family Dancing*, Leavitt's widely acclaimed first collection, four deal overtly or implicitly with homosexual relationships that are a source of either anxiety or discord; three concern mothers who are afflicted with cancer and the effects of their illness on their children; and in some of these as well as others, families that were once close-knit disintegrate when the father divorces the mother to marry another woman or, in one case, to move in with his homosexual lover. In a particularly bizarre story called "Aliens" a father, disturbed by a family quarrel, deliberately drives his car over an embankment and as a result loses an eye and the ability to speak. His children are a boy who is a computer prodigy obsessed with his software, and a girl who is convinced that she is an alien from the planet Abdur—both in effect self-created aliens who have exiled themselves from the family tragedy.

Along with homosexuality, which later becomes an increasingly large preoccupation in his work, Leavitt's most dependable subject thus seems to be domestic unhappiness. But he tends to treat it as a fait accompli, as something that is simply endemic to family life, rather than as a condition arising from specific faults of incompatibility that can be explored and understood through a close examination of his characters. As a rule, Leavitt stops short of making such an examination. Nevertheless, because domestic unhappiness is, after all, the product of conflict, however unexamined, it does provide his stories with a dramatic tension they would not otherwise have. Yet there are just so many ways that people can be affected by it, and after a time his representations of those ways begin to read like a collection of virtually interchangeable case histories designed for use in a sociology course on "Marriage and the Family." Unhappy families, to contradict Tolstoy, finally become all alike. They are unhappy but no longer each in its own way. Misery is their universal condition. But unless the misery is particularized and shown to vary from case to case, it fails to function as a characterizing condition and serves only to emphasize their sameness.

Most of the characters in Leavitt's novel *The Lost Language of Cranes* are also miserable, and they are mostly miserable in the same way and about the same thing—their homosexuality. The novel is all about failed homosexual relationships, and it is about virtually nothing else. The characters are portrayed exclusively in terms of their sexual orientation. Other aspects of their lives—jobs, cultural interests, hobbies, other people who are not principal figures in the sexual ballet, the New York City environment through which they move and cruise—these are merely stage decorations for the central drama involving the search for the attention and love of other men and the incessant anguish generated by the search.

If this were a story of conventional heterosexual romance, it would be dismissed as being hopelessly banal and predictable. The lovers would either consummate their passion and live happily ever after, or they would discover that they had nothing in common but their passion and so would separate and live to lust another day. But here there is dramatic complication arising from the existence in some social quarters of the taboo against homosexuality, and this gives rise to the question, which the characters endlessly discuss, whether or not to go public with one's sexual preferences, in particular whether to come out to one's parents and suffer the consequences.

As the novel demonstrates, the consequences can either be relatively benign or deeply dire, ranging from reluctant acceptance to violent banishment forever from the family circle. But in the case of the novel's young protagonist, Philip Benjamin, there is the happy circumstance that his father is himself a closet gay, has lived for years in deep torment over the fact, and is finally able, in the final scene of the novel, to acknowledge a common bond with his son by daring to come out to him. This is the gimmick on which the entire novel is constructed, and while it surely must represent the fulfillment of every young homosexual's most cherished fantasy, it is scarcely acceptable as either true to life or good for the novel, which in other respects has some real literary merit.

The portrait of the male homosexual experience that

Leavitt presents is either callow in the extreme or, if accurate, depressingly bleak. The attraction between man and man appears to be almost exclusively genital-centered. The men he describes, all of whom are ostensibly searching for companionship and love, have only sexual contact, either in porno theaters and gay bars or at home in bed, and appear to be incapable of developing any deeper relationships based upon other qualities such as shared interests or some more exalted communion of kindred souls. The sex act, whether oral, anal, or mutually masturbatory, is the be all and end all of their relationships, and apparently it matters scarcely at all whether the act is performed with friend or total stranger. Again, if a heterosexual relationship were described in these terms, as based exclusively on sexual intercourse, it would be judged to be either very short-lived or from the beginning empty.

Mr. Leavitt is, like so many of his well-trained contemporaries, an accomplished writer of prose. But if he is to use his considerable gifts to become something more than a slick proselytizer for gay rights, he will need to broaden his range and his sympathies and come to understand that sexual orientation is not by itself a sufficient basis for the creation of meaningful portraits of the immensely complicated human condition.

▪ II ▪

Lorrie Moore also writes about unhappy relationships, but she is such a fine writer that she could as easily write about happy ones and they would not be all alike. This is because she does with apparent ease what so few of her contemporaries seem able to do: She individualizes her characters so that each is clearly and understandably unhappy in his or, in Moore's case, mostly her own way.

Moore's particular concern is with the anxieties generated among single young women by the effort to create and then sustain relationships with men who are afflicted with the contemporary masculine fear of commitment, who take but cannot give, and who are otherwise unworthy objects of the female hunger for intimacy and love. In other words, Moore's stories are primarily chronicles of the process by which hopeful yet cynical young women carry on the search for the proverbial and forever elusive Mr. Right. And taken together they form a very clear and often very devastating account of the courtship rituals of unmarried adults in the 1970s and 1980s, people of good will and the best intentions who, for personal reasons or because of their position in history, apparently lack access to the traditional means of validating relationship such as the presence of high passion, compatibility of habits and values, or the magical meeting of kindred minds, and so are obliged to discover new ones as they go along—if, indeed, new ones are to be found.

In one of her best early stories, "How to Be an Other Woman," Moore offers a kind of tragicomic catalogue of the various phases of this process. The young female narrator meets an attractive potential lover, and they begin to go out together. She tells us that "after four movies, three concerts, and two-and-a-half museums, you sleep with him. It seems the right number of cultural events"—not, significantly, events that, as they multiply, serve to deepen intimacy between the two or to stimulate an increasing desire to share that intimacy in bed. Rather, the number of occasions of contact simply accumulate like supermarket green stamps to the point where, mathematically, sex and bed are indicated.

Predictably, the affair proceeds and goes nowhere. The couple meet periodically and sleep together. But it turns out that he is not only married but has all along been involved with another woman not his wife. In addition, he proves to be emotionally and spiritually something of a clod. So the relationship gradually peters out, a pattern that becomes standard in nearly all the stories Moore devotes to the subject. Over and over again the problem seems to be that the men and women in her world simply do not feel or care very much for one another. They may need each other momentarily. They may want, or think they want, true love from each other. But the most they seem to get is a failure of communication and poor sex.

Perhaps it is for this reason that Moore seems able to describe relationships only as they begin and as they end. She appears to have no sense of what lies in between, what the *substance* of relationship might be or what elements might cause it to begin but sustain it so that it does not have to end. And that just may be her point: that there is somehow an implicit hollowness at the core of such provisional liaisons in our time, an absence of some necessary power of trust, loyalty, and commitment on the part of two people who, without such power, move through the phases of courtship as if they were taking courses in togetherness that in time will earn them enough credits for a degree in happiness. That is the sadness of their condition, and it is the dominant mood of just about everything Moore has written, even those stories that have nothing to do with unhappy relationships.

In "Go Like This," for example, a young woman discovers that she has terminal cancer and plans to commit what she calls "rational suicide." Early in the story she twice mentions Tolstoy's Ivan Ilych, and the reference, fairly or unfairly, invites a comparison between his story and hers, particularly since the contrast effectively defines the dimension of meaning that is missing from her world.

Ivan Ilych has lived a perfectly decorous life in strict conformity to the rules of propriety laid down by nineteenth-century Russian bourgeois society. He has been an extremely successful magistrate, has, in fact, subordinated all other aspects of his existence to the fulfillment of his professional duties. "In all this the thing was to exclude everything fresh and vital, which always disturbs the regular course of official business, and to admit only official relations with people, and then only on official grounds."

But as Ivan Ilych lies dying of cancer, he thinks back over his life and realizes, first, that everything that has happened to him since childhood has brought him steadily diminishing satisfactions. "It is as if I had been going downhill while I imagined I was going up. And that is really what it was. I was going up in public opinion, but to the same extent life was ebbing away from me." Finally he is driven to ask himself the fateful question, "Maybe I did not live as I ought to have done. . . . But how could that be, when I did everything properly?" "And whenever the thought occurred to him . . . that it all resulted from his not having lived as he ought to have done, he at once recalled the correctness of his whole life and dismissed so strange an idea."

But as his suffering grows more severe, Ivan Ilych is no longer able to dismiss this strange idea and is forced to the extremely bleak conclusion that all he has lived for is falsehood and deception, that, in fact, his whole life has been a lie.

His story, in short, becomes not only a tragic study of the unexamined life examined too late to be remedied but a deeply subversive ironic critique of the moral and emotional impoverishment that can result from blind conformity to the official values of the established culture.

By contrast, the narrator of Moore's story never achieves and apparently has never possessed any sort of critical perspective on either her life or her culture. She accepts without question the conventional values of her class and time and seems never to have imagined an alternative to them. When she decides to commit suicide, she brings together a forum of her friends and submits the idea to their collective psychological arbitration, not realizing that she is enacting a sad parody of the kind of group-therapy approach to crisis that has served to trivialize contemporary emotional life and, in her case, to deprive her of what would otherwise have been that critical moment of anguished decision when one is, or should be, left alone to choose one's fate. But, said Yeats, "we begin to live when we have conceived life as tragedy," and this Ivan Ilych does, and she does not do, presumably because the terms of tragedy are missing from her world. When at last she is ready to take the fatal dose of sleeping pills, she does not think about the meaning of her life but wonders instead who will take her daughter to clarinet class and which woman among her friends her husband will sleep with after she is dead.

Moore is often described as a comic writer, but obviously her comedy does not arise from her subject matter. Rather, it is almost entirely verbal. She is deeply addicted to the creation of clever and often very bad puns, zany one-liners, and other ludicrous dislocations of language. But seen in relation to her altogether unfunny materials, it becomes clear that her humor is actually a kind of sublimated scream, "gaiety transfiguring all that dread," as Yeats also said, anxiety displaced into jokes that Moore and her characters incessantly make but at which no one is laughing. It is also clear that her puns in particular represent a rather bitter comment on the fact that language is no longer effective as a means by which people can cure their helpless inability to communicate with one another.

In the story called "What Is Seized" a young woman suffering from this inability studies her mother's scrapbook in the hope of finding some clue to what may once have been an authentic language of love. But then her mother informs her that her father was a cold man. "Even his I love you's were like tiny daggers." Thus, even the most conventional and supposedly dependable language proves to be untrustworthy, and the daughter is left extremely reluctant to take the risks of love. "And I say to myself I will leave every cold man, every man for whom music is some private physics and love some unstoppable dance. I will try to make them regret."

But then throughout Moore's fiction her characters repeatedly try and fail to find the right language with which to express their feelings. Words, with their approximate definitions and multiple implications, become useless. Men and women struggle to communicate with one another. But the assumptions behind their words are often so radically different that they might as well be speaking in an incomprehensible foreign language. In "How to Be an Other Woman" the narrator turns to the man in her bed and says, "Usually I don't like discussing sex, but . . . ," to which he replies, "I don't like disgusting sex, either," and falls asleep. This kind of frustration leads the protagonist of the story called "To Fill" to ask herself, "What are the speaking terms and am I on them with anyone?"

In Moore's first novel, fittingly entitled *Anagrams*, there is no developing action because nothing accrues, nothing the characters do or say gets effectively done or successfully said. It is all a dread-launched documentation of all the ways it is possible not to communicate with others or with one's self. Significantly, the main character, a woman named Benna, is preoccupied with wordplay, with trying to reinvent language, with finding new combinations of letters, new interpretations, anything that will endow words with meaning. Her obsession with creating bad puns and anagrams is, in fact, an index of her despair because in each case the rearranged letters spell out something ugly or ominous. *Gutless* becomes *guilts; lovesick* becomes *evil louse; bedroom* becomes *boredom.* Wherever Benna goes, she makes puns that underscore her sadness. "When you walk through a store hold your head up high . . ." "Walk on, walk on, with holes in your heart." Her lover sees her tossing pillows across the room and asks, "What are you doing?" "Throwing cushion to the winds," she replies. "Meaning, if it existed at all, was unstable and could not survive the slightest reshuffling of letters. One gust of wind and *Santa* becomes *Satan*."

Benna and her friend Eleanor, both of whom are small-time academics, use their reshuffled language as a kind of secret code that separates them from, and at the same time elevates them above, other people, even as they hunger for connection with them. Benna says that she has given Eleanor an unusual double appointment: Gym and Anguish-as-a-Second-Language. Every time Eleanor passes the departmental sign for "outgoing mail," she mutters, "I've had enough of those; I need a wan poet type." The two women have managed to barricade themselves inside their private lexicon of frustration and loneliness, and the cause of it all is unlocatable, therefore incurable. All Benna has to sustain her is her wordplay and her extremely inventive fantasy life. In fact, it is possible that Eleanor exists only as a wish-fulfillment of her need for an intimate friend, and there is even reason to suppose that the adorable six-year-old daughter who is such excellent company for Benna may live only in her anguished imagination.

One sees Moore throughout her work struggling to define exactly what has gone wrong with the world and with human relationships, what the premises of existence have become. And there are moments when her excellent prose seems to be bouncing frantically off walls as it searches for some clarifying truth that she knows must exist, but that, like her characters, she cannot find the language to describe. Yet even though ultimate answers elude her, Moore remains one of the most sensitive and articulate chroniclers of what it feels like to be alive and overly vulnerable to life in these final somber years of the twentieth century. She takes one inside the quaking nervous systems of people who are lone survivors, wounded, frightened, and too acutely conscious of their aloneness, their need, and their inability to do much of anything to help themselves. One can only hope that her mordant sense of humor will protect Moore from the worst effects of the dark troubles she so clearly perceives.

CHAPTER V

CAMEOS OF THE BIZARRE

Like Moore, T. Coraghessan Boyle is an acerbically witty writer. But where Moore's comic vision is expressed primarily through her irreverent observations on the contemporary social scene as well as through the self-protective wordplay of her characters, his is embodied and objectified in his fictional situations, his absurd, outrageously bizarre plots. Moore is, in short, a writer of satirical realism, while Boyle is a gothic fabulist writing in the tradition of what used to be called "black humor." And one of his several distinctions is that in his stories, if not his novels, he has brought new vitality to that moribund form at the same time that he has shown himself to be a precocious master of its most macabre and mesmerizing effects. His imaginative range and power of invention appear to be limitless, and no other writer of his generation begins to equal him in sheer eloquence and richness of language.

Since Boyle is a remarkably consistent writer, examples of the excellence of his prose can be found just about anywhere in his work. Here are three passages chosen at random:

> I've always been a quitter. I quit the Boy Scouts, the glee club, the marching band. Gave up my paper route,

turned my back on the church, stuffed the basketball team. I dropped out of college, sidestepped the army with a 4-F on the grounds of mental instability, went back to school, made a go of it, entered a Ph.D. program in nineteenth-century British literature, sat in the front row, took notes assiduously, bought a pair of horn-rims, and quit on the eve of my comprehensive exams. I got married, separated, divorced. Quit smoking, quit jogging, quit eating red meat. I quit jobs: digging graves, pumping gas, selling insurance, showing pornographic films in an art theater in Boston. When I was nineteen I made frantic love to a pinch-faced, sack-bosomed girl I'd known from high school. She got pregnant. I quit town. About the only thing I didn't give up on was the summer camp. . . . Let me tell you about it.

I don't know what it was exactly—the impulse toward preservation in the face of flux, some natal fascination with girth—who can say? But suddenly, in the winter of my thirty-first year, I was seized with an overmastering desire to seek out the company of whales. That's right: whales. Flukes and blowholes. Leviathan. Moby Dick.

There was a blizzard in the Dakotas, an earthquake in Chile, and a solar eclipse over most of the Northern Hemisphere the day I stepped up to the governor's podium in Des Moines and announced my candidacy for the highest post in the land. As the lunar shadow crept over the Midwest like a stain in water, as noon became night and the creatures of the earth fell into an unnatural frenzy and the birds of the air fled to premature roosts, I stood in a puddle of TV lights, Lorna at my side, and calmly raked the incumbent over the coals.

> It was a nice campaign ploy—I think I used the term "penumbra" half a dozen times in my speech—but beyond that I really didn't attach too much significance to the whole thing. I wasn't superstitious. I wore no chains or amulets. I'd never had a rabbit's foot. I attended church only because my constituents expected me to. Of portents, I knew nothing.

These are all opening paragraphs, and they each convey a message rarely found in the work of Boyle's contemporaries: that there is actually a story of some real interest about to be told, that it is to be told by an expert, and that in this beginning is contained an important clue to the story's meaning and outcome. Thus, in the first, the narrator's history of failure is a clear prediction of some climactic future failure. In the second, there is the promise of some culminating encounter with whales, and in the third, a subtle hint of some weird connection between the Presidency and the moon.

Ideally in fiction, the ending should always be foreshadowed in the beginning. But for that to happen, the writer must be from the start in complete command of his materials, and that Boyle obviously is. He is also notable for the great authority of his narrative voice, and the precision and resonance of the language in which that voice is expressed. It is a language that is not only highly literate but unusually literary in the sense that it seems to derive from an intellectual culture which has somehow escaped the impoverishment that has debilitated the language of so many of the writers I have discussed. In reading Boyle one feels in close touch with a mind enriched by long exposure to literature, while in the case of some others of his generation, one has the strong impression that one is reading writers who have read few books they did not write themselves. The extent to which Boyle has been able to apply in his fiction a literary knowledge that they seem not to possess may be seen most clearly in his use of descriptive detail, which is always dynamically functional and never merely decorative as it tends so often to be in the work, for example, of Ann Beattie and Frederick Barthelme. Details for them seem to represent window dressing or incremental props gathered to furnish out the vacuum that should be occupied by drama and characterization. And they frequently make one feel that they begin to write, holding in their heads a cornucopia of assorted details, and hope that if they keep writing long enough, they will find something that they can use them to describe. Boyle, on the other hand, appears to know exactly what he wants to describe before he begins to write, and the details he uses to describe it are the precise verbal enactments of his thorough conception of his subject.

Yet, interestingly enough, what Boyle chooses to describe is in every respect antithetical to the fine discriminations and focused authority that are the features of his literary style. The world he repeatedly evokes in his stories is one in which no authoritative standards any longer exist for distinguishing between the plausibly real and the diabolically fantastic, the benevolent and the malevolent, the ridiculous and the dreadful. To read through the various collections of his short fiction is to travel through a Grand Guignol of death masks and leering false faces and a populace made up of assorted psychopaths, rapists, tormentors, and crazed incarnations of the Devil. Subversion, betrayal, and random disaster, along with perverse and unfathomable happenings, threaten constantly to sabotage the fragile sanities of what most people consider normal life.

In the title story of *Descent of Man*, Boyle's first collection, the narrator's girlfriend working at a primate research center falls in love and copulates with a chimpanzee who is a genius and has translated Darwin's *Descent of Man*, Chomsky's *Language and Mind*, and Nietzsche's *Beyond Good and Evil* into Yerkish. He has also written three operas. A story called "The Champ" is constructed on the parodic format of a championship boxing match, but the two contestants are actually competing for the world's eating championship. At the start of the match in the Madison Square Garden arena, the referee instructs the two men to "touch midriffs and come out eating." And near the end, as the champion for thirty-seven years is about to go down in defeat, his mother rises up among the spectators and calls out, "Clean your plate." This inspires him to extra effort and he outeats his opponent with bowls of gruel, his favorite boyhood food.

Among the stories that follow in the collection and in *Greasy Lake* and *If the River Was Whiskey*, another parody, this one of the "Lassie" television series, allows the faithful collie to abandon Timmy at a fateful moment and run off with a sexy coyote stud. In other stories, a heavy rain turns out to be blood; Idi Amin Dada comes to New York to take part in the Second International Dada Fair; a restaurant created exclusively for women is invaded by a man in drag; a man is held prisoner in a mammoth auto service garage, waiting perhaps forever for his car to be repaired; a collector of rare objects develops a passion for collecting beer cans; a scientific genius has a son whose mother is a sow and breeds a new variety of cats that neither defecate nor micturate; an obese boy rapes a naked, sunbathing girl on a beach; Dwight D. Eisenhower and Nina Khrushchev carry on a secret love affair; in the story quoted from earlier, an Iowa governor is elected President because he promises to put a new moon into orbit around the earth (the old one looks cheesy); a woman obsessed with hygiene insists that her lover wear a full-body condom; a deeply disturbed adopted son newly released from prison stalks his foster parents with a hive of killer bees; and a stockbroker, heavily in debt, makes a fatal bargain with the Devil.

The trouble with these brilliantly written and imagined stories is that they are largely autotelic. Nearly all of them are simply about themselves, have reference to very little beyond themselves, and tend to substitute an extreme eccentricity of plot for characterization and thematic significance. Boyle does, to be sure, make some effort in a few of the stories to address satirically certain particularly ludicrous features of contemporary life—our national paranoia about germs in the full-body condom story, the rabid feminism that creates the women-only restaurant.

But his problem seems to be that perhaps because absolutely everything interests him, he has so far failed to discover his single compelling subject. He has not been able, as Scott Fitzgerald once said about Thomas Wolfe, "to line himself up along a solid gold bar, like Hemingway's courage or Joseph Conrad's art or D. H. Lawrence's intense cohabitations." Until he does and is also able to bring his extraordinary talents more completely into alignment with the significant issues of his time, Boyle seems destined to remain a writer hamstrung by his very inventiveness and versatility and condemned to go on producing small, perfect cameos of grotesque action that startle and entertain but do not edify or instruct.

■ CHAPTER VI ■

DECOR VAPIDITY, DESIGNER MURDER

■

Ever since the appearance of his first novel, *Bright Lights, Big City,* in 1984, Jay McInerney has been the recipient of far more publicity than is good for a young writer of promise. Perhaps because he lives a life in New York that is scarcely distinguishable from that of his characters, he has been taken up and rather extravagantly fawned upon by the gossip columnists, interviewed in all the news media, regularly photographed at parties and nightclubs, usually in the company of fashion models or fashionable literary friends and editors, and he has even endured the distinction of being pilloried at length in print by his former wife.

McInerney has, in other words, experienced the best and worst effects of the kind of golden boy celebrity once enjoyed by the young Scott Fitzgerald and J. D. Salinger. In fact, these are the writers with whom he has been repeatedly compared, and if one does not look too closely, the comparison seems quite apt. The three men all wrote first novels that either reflected the manners and morals of their respective generations or, as happened in the case of *The Catcher in the Rye*, were recognized by their generations as telling some essential truth about them. But the similarity ends there, and the fact that it does is a measure of the limitations of McInerney's vision when assessed in relation to the larger and more complex vision of his distinguished predecessors.

This Side of Paradise and *The Catcher in the Rye* are both novels of initiation in the sense that they have to do with youthful confrontations for the first time with certain potentially educative experiences. But they are also novels in which the central motivation is the search for authenticity, whether it is to be found among the people Holden Caulfield encounters in his desperate odyssey through the jungles of New York or in Amory Blaine's naively romantic relationships with various women. But in the case of both men the search is conducted against the pressure of a strong moral reticence to be taken in and forced to settle for less than the absolutely genuine. This is to say that even as each of their stories represents a portrait of a younger generation, each is also a critical examination of the premises on which the way of life of that generation is conducted. Salinger's prose style is the very embodiment in language of Holden's sternly monitory fastidiousness, his refusal to tolerate those who show the slightest evidence of belonging to his personal *Index Prohibitorum* of phonies, bores, deceivers, and perverts. "If you really want to hear about it," he says at the beginning of the novel, "the first thing you'll probably want to know is where I was born, and what my lousy childhood was like, and how my parents were occupied and all before they had me, and all that David Copperfield kind of crap." In short, the opening message is that you probably don't *really* want to hear about it but are only pretending that you do. But if you want to hear about it, there will be no fancy lies in the manner of the telling, no effort made to be literary, because the traditional conventions of narrative evade, disguise, or prettify the truth and are, therefore, crap.

In his own search for authenticity of feeling Amory Blaine takes a softer line because his attitude is more ambiguous and he lacks Holden's dogmatic conviction. What he does have is an innocent romantic infatuation with wealth, social position, and beauty, particularly the beauty of women, at the same time that what is left of his or Fitzgerald's lapsed-Catholic conscience causes him to meditate on the darker implications of the very values he so extravagantly admires.

"Amory saw girls doing things," says Fitzgerald, "that even in his memory would have been impossible: eating three-o'clock, after-dance suppers in impossible cafés, talking of every side of life with an air half of earnestness, half of mockery, yet with a furtive excitement that Amory considered stood for a real moral letdown. But he never realized how widespread it was until he saw the cities between New York and Chicago as one vast juvenile intrigue." Amory is clearly fascinated by the girls and the atmosphere of intrigue. But he is also shocked by the girls' departure from maidenly decorum, a sure sign of "real moral letdown." Like the solitary watcher in *The Great Gatsby*, Amory is both "within and without, simultaneously enchanted and repelled."

Exactly what causes Amory's repulsion is never fully understood either by him or apparently by Fitzgerald. But it is expressed in a series of thematically undigested episodes and amateurish images that recur throughout the novel and obviously stem from some deep-seated sexual guilt.

Early in the novel, when Amory is still in prep school, he and a girlfriend find themselves alone in a "little den" upstairs at the country club. There they kiss, "their lips brush[ing] like young wild flowers in the wind." But "sudden revulsion seized Amory, disgust, loathing for the whole incident," and he "desired frantically to be away." Later as a student at Princeton he goes with a classmate and two girls on a Broadway holiday. Toward the end of the evening after they arrive at the girls' apartment, he is again overcome by loathing, this time for the decadent atmosphere of the place and his female partner's "sidelong, suggestive smile" and for a terrifying moment he sees a deathlike figure sitting opposite him on the divan. Still later, when he, a friend, and a girl are caught in a hotel room by house detectives, Amory sees above the body of the girl sobbing on the bed "an aura, gossamer as a moonbeam, tainted as stale, weak wine, yet a horror, diffusely brooding . . . and over by the window among the stirring curtains stood something else, featureless and indistinguishable, yet strangely familiar." This mysterious presence, like the deathlike figure, is evidently another incarnation of the strange man who, in an earlier scene, follows Amory and who appears to be wearing no shoes, "but, instead, a sort of half moccasin, pointed, though, like the shoes they wore in the fourteenth century, and with the little ends curling up. They were a darkish brown and his toes seemed to fill them to the end. . . . They were unutterably terrible."

These ominous, accusatory apparitions, treated so awkwardly in *This Side of Paradise*, foreshadow the far more powerful image of the enormous painted eyes of Dr. T. J. Eckleburg that gaze coldly out over the moral wasteland setting of *The Great Gatsby* and that perhaps represent the condemnatory judgment of God. Whether or not such effects are the products of Catholic conscience or sexual guilt or both, they are expressive of Fitzgerald's acute moral sense, his remarkable sensitivity to the strong potential for tragedy that lay just beneath the shining surfaces of the glamour and careless extravagance that, with another part of himself, he so deeply admired in the life of his generation. This sensitivity made it possible for him to produce such extraordinary novels as *The Great Gatsby* and *Tender Is the Night* in which the tragic consequences of irresponsible or exploitative behavior in a setting of great wealth and privilege are fully dramatized. It also enabled him at a very young age to create in *This Side of Paradise* something far more substantial than a shallow and merely documentary portrait of the manners and morals of American Jazz Age youth.

Bright Lights, Big City is just such a portrait of a much later generation of American youth, and it is so because, unlike Salinger, Fitzgerald, and even his contemporary, Lorrie Moore, McInerney evidently possesses no morally evaluative or critical attitude toward his materials. His characters are all young, presumably attractive, mostly very affluent people who float through the fashionable nightspots of New York without a thought in their heads, seemingly indifferent to or unconscious of their environment, seeking no authenticity beyond sex, entertainment, and cocaine anesthesia. There is nothing to indicate that they have arrived at this condition because they are members of some new hedonistic cult or are in flight from some deeply traumatic past experience. They are simply *there,* and neither they nor McInerney seems to know or care why or how they got there. He apparently conceives of no alternative to their way of life, and he does not seem the least bit aware of its incredible vapidity.

With no past history and no consciousness of their present condition, his characters are distinguishable from one another not by their degrees of intelligence, charm, learning, or wit but by their patterns of consumership, by what they wear, eat, and drink and where they eat and drink. But since they all wear the same designer clothes and eat and drink in the same restaurants and bars, they are not really distinguishable from one another at all. For as a woman in Bret Easton Ellis's novel *American Psycho* says about the same society, "Everybody's rich, everybody's good-looking, everybody has a great body," which is to suggest that people are themselves designer products self-created by income, cosmetics, diet, and exercise and are, therefore, interchangeable, even consumable, a fact that, as I shall later show, comes to have in Ellis's novel extremely sinister implications.

In *Bright Lights, Big City* there is nothing that is sinister but much that is boring about the monotonous uniformity of the characters' appearance, habits, conversation, and activities, yet that is the primary substance of the book. In a sense it is a novel of contemporary social manners in which the manners are the principal protagonist, and the characters are merely decor figures designed to display them. But unlike the traditional novel of manners, in which often very subtle gradations of class status and cultural background function both to characterize people and to dramatize their relationships, here there is only status based on the kind of superficial knowledge that enables one to distinguish between what is fashionable at the moment and what is not. And since all the people in the novel possess such knowledge in the same degree, it does not operate either to characterize or dramatize them but simply to deepen the effect of their interchangeability. There is also among them no Holden Caulfield to raise the question of the phoniness of their way of life, no Amory Blaine to assess the destructive potential of the values of promiscuous consumership on which it is based, and, unfortunately, McInerney supplies neither perspective.

It is not surprising that the only discernible emotions generated in the novel are boredom and depression. When one is not drunk, up or out on cocaine, or having sex, one is bored and depressed. And most of the time when one *is* drunk, on cocaine, or having sex, one is bored and depressed. The appropriately nameless young male protagonist is bored and depressed through virtually the whole of the novel. He is especially depressed because his beautiful, fashion-model wife has abruptly left him for reasons he is unable to fathom, and he is both bored and depressed by the job he has as a fact-checker on the staff of a *New Yorker*–style magazine. Most of the action concerns his efforts to escape being depressed over the departure of his wife and the dullness of his job by going incessantly to restaurants and parties and trying to take as many women to bed as he possibly can. Finally, he manages to get himself fired from his job, and after encountering his wife at a party, to come to terms with the fact that she has left him. After all, she was not very bright in the first place. As his friend Tad Allagash has earlier pointed out, she had a sign on her forehead that said, "Space to Let. Long and Short Term Leasing."

At the end of *This Side of Paradise* Amory proclaims to the world, "I know myself but that is all." Of course he does not know himself at all. But the important thing is that *we* know him. He has been, however clumsily, created as a character. But when McInerney's young man decides at the end of a long, exhausting round of all-night partying that he "will have to learn everything all over again," we can only assume he means that he will try now to find a way to stop being depressed. But as I suggested earlier, depression alone is not an effective characterizing agent, if only because a depressed person does not become a character. He becomes his condition.

McInerney's next novel about the New York youth scene, *Story of My Life*, is something of a stylistic tour de force because it is told from the point of view and in the quaint colloquial language of a bright but poorly educated young woman named Alison Poole. Alison's talk is studded with locutions like "I go" instead of "I say," "in lust with" instead of "in love with," and "I am not a happy unit," as indeed she is not. Her tone throughout is a mixture of irritability and cynical mockery in which she expresses her conviction that bad things have happened to her in the past and will surely happen again, that nothing is what it seems to be, and that really she could not care less. But of course she does care. She enters into each of her lust affairs, of which there are a great many, with a tarnished but still wistful hope that this time she will find love. Instead she discovers only that she is "in lust" and that her various sex partners are really boys, not men, who always disappoint her in some way.

In New York Alison shares an apartment with a friend from childhood, a woman named Jeannie, and studies acting at the Lee Strasberg Studio. However, since her rich father frequently fails to send her tuition money, her attendance at class is sporadic. Yet it would probably be sporadic in any case because, in spite of her brash assertiveness, Alison is oddly passive and easily distracted. She has several girlfriends, all of whom are rich and beautiful, and when they insist that she go out with them to parties or nightclubs or spend the night sniffing cocaine, she complies even when it means that she will be unable to get up for class the next day.

The world Alison inhabits is one in which everything is possible; therefore, nothing is imperative. All problems can be solved through the application of some money to the affected areas. When the rent on the apartment is not paid and she and Jeannie are about to be evicted, Jeannie's father can be coerced into giving them money, or a former lover can be blackmailed into giving it when Alison lies to him that she is pregnant. When she actually does become pregnant, there are grandmother's pearls to be sold to pay for an abortion. Since at least one of her rich friends always has some money, drugs can always be bought, and affluent boyfriends are always good for meals in the best restaurants.

In fact, so far as Alison and her women friends are concerned, men in general are commodities to be used either for money or for sex. They are mostly interchangeable, although some have more money and better bodies than others and can be ranked on a scale of one to ten on the basis of their fiscal generosity, their athletic prowess in bed, and the size of their penises. Sex and drugs, along with money, are the only real sources of satisfaction, and very often at cocaine parties the chief recreation is a game called "Truth or Dare," in which a person is required either to tell what he or she honestly thinks of another person (Does a woman rank one of the men present a ten in bed?) or is obliged to take the dare, which usually involves taking one's clothes off. It is a game that is pursued with great dedication and is always accompanied by great hilarity.

Most of the novel consists of an absolutely deadpan documentation of these and similar activities. It is all quite skillfully done, and Alison's narrative style is really quite charming. But again as happened in *Bright Lights, Big City,* McInerney fails to place her way of life in critical perspective, nor does he suggest that there might be some less infantile alternative to it. Since all material problems can be solved with money, and no moral or ethical problems are ever encountered, the elements essential to the creation of dramatic significance are missing from the novel. There is no final effect of either pathos or tragedy, even when Alison suffers a drug overdose and is confined in a sanitarium. Holden Caulfield also ends his story in a sanitarium, but one feels that he at least has genuinely suffered, has done honorable battle with forces that pose a real threat to his innocent integrity, and so has engaged our sympathy and respect. Alison, on the other hand, remains at the end as remote, unaffected, and, therefore, as uncreated as she was at the beginning.

▪ II ▪

Like *Bright Lights, Big City*, Bret Easton Ellis's *Less Than Zero* is a highly acclaimed first novel written in this case by a young man barely into his twenties. It also shares with McInerney's novel the same working assumption or presumption: that the intellectual and emotional blankness of a certain class of the affluent young is so profoundly fascinating that it deserves to be examined at book length.

Surely, no other novel in recent history—not even McInerney's—has concerned material that is indeed so much less than zero in dramatic content and thematic meaning. At the very least a book about people who cannot think or feel had better provide some clue as to the reason they cannot think or feel—unless of course one assumes, as Ellis may well have done, that this is such a universal human condition in our time that it no longer requires an explanation. But back when Hemingway wrote *The Sun Also Rises* and the condition was not yet entirely universal, he made certain that his readers understood early in the novel exactly what influences had formed his characters: that Jake Barnes had been grievously wounded in his sexual capacity by the war and so was impotent and embittered, that Brett Ashley had lost her true love in the war, could not sleep with Jake, and was alcoholic and promiscuous because she no longer cared very much about anything, and that Robert Cohn was a romantic fool who had acquired his sentimental vision of life through reading the wrong books and simply did not realize that he was trying to impose on people standards of feeling that the war had rendered obsolete. All the characters in the novel were, in one way or another, casualties, and their behavior was the direct result of their wounded condition.

Ellis's characters also behave as if they were casualties but evidently just because they have not been wounded. They inhabit an environment that imposes upon them no challenge or risk of any kind, that is able instantly to satisfy their every wish without the expenditure of the slightest effort on their part, that provides them with all the money they need to buy the most expensive luxuries and the freedom to consume drugs, sex, cars, parties, discos, and restaurants without any limits on the degree of their consumption.

The central characters of the novel are all young and attractive and their fathers are all extremely ambitious and wealthy film executives whose money the young people freely spend but whose ambition they would not dream of emulating, partly because they find it rather vulgar but mainly because they have nothing to strive for. As a rule, their parents are divorced, and their mothers have taken up with younger men, while the fathers have married younger women or are having affairs with younger men. All of them live in large mansions with gates that open onto spacious grounds.

Ellis's narrator-protagonist is a young man named Clay, and the novel begins with his arrival in Los Angeles from some school in New Hampshire to spend four weeks over Christmas with his family and friends. His narrative tone is almost uniformly affectless except at those occasional moments when he confesses to feeling vaguely ill. But one does not know whether this is the result of the drugs and alcohol he constantly consumes or is meant to be a symptom of his faint distaste for the kind of life he and his friends cannot help but lead. Most of the time he just floats through the endless series of identical parties, the meetings with friends and drug dealers, and the meals at restaurants, barely sentient enough to notice who was present and what, if anything, was said and done. But he is nearly always unable to remember what happened the night before.

Where McInerney's young people at least seemed to enjoy

their cocaine and sex, Clay and his friends clearly do not. They merely use them as a brief diversion from their blankness in order to experience another kind of blankness. When Clay spends the night with Blair, his girlfriend from the time before he left for school, he gives this account of the morning after:

> I'm lying in Blair's bed. . . . I feel something hard and covered with fur and I reach under myself and it's this stuffed black cat. I drop it on the floor and then get up and take a shower. . . Blair's smoking a cigarette and watching MTV, the sound turned down low.
>
> "Will you call me before Christmas?" she asks.
>
> "Maybe." I pull on my vest, wondering why I even came here in the first place.
>
> "You've still got my number, don't you?" . . .
>
> "Yeah, Blair. I've got your number. I'll get in touch." . . .
>
> "If I don't see you before Christmas," she stops. "Have a good one."
>
> I look at her a moment. "Hey, you too." . . .
>
> I step out the door and start to close it.
>
> "Clay?" she whispers loudly.
>
> I stop but don't turn around. "Yeah?"
>
> "Nothing."

So much for erotic passion.

In an earlier scene Clay has a conversation with his mother, during which she asks him what he wants for Christmas. "Nothing," he replies. Then he asks her what she wants, and she says, "I don't know. I just want to have a nice Christmas." Then she says, "You look unhappy," and he says, "You do too," "hoping that she won't say anything else. She doesn't say anything else, until she's finished her third glass of wine and poured her fourth."

"How was the party?" [she asks.]
"Okay." . . .
She takes a swallow of wine. "What time did you leave it?"
"I don't remember."
"One? Two?"
"Must of been one."
"Oh." She pauses again and takes another swallow.
"It wasn't very good," I say, looking at her.
"Why?" she asks, curious.
"It just wasn't," I say and look back at my hands.

No history is given for this exchange, no hint that there is no longer feeling between mother and son because some monstrous domestic crisis has alienated them from each other. In the midst of their plethora of riches, they are simply miserable, and that is that.

There are three occasions in the novel when some dramatic tension is generated and then only because extreme ugliness is encountered. One is a scene in which Clay and some of his friends find a dead body in an alley behind a disco. A young boy has evidently been beaten to death or perhaps he has died of a drug overdose. Two girls who have seen the body are giggling, and one of them says, "We gotta bring Marcia. She'll freak out." Rip, one of Clay's friends, "jabs the boy in the stomach with his foot."

"Sure he's dead?"

"See him moving?"

Rip "sticks a cigarette in the boy's mouth. We stand there for five more minutes. Then Spin stands up and shakes his head . . . and says, 'Man, I need a cigarette.' "

"Rip gets up and holds onto my arm and says to me and Trent, 'Listen, you two, you've gotta come over to my place.' "

So much for the spectacle of death, which, like the discos,

parties, famous restaurants, and expensive cars, is just another element of the environmental decor, something that provides brief diversion, is used, passed through, and left behind.

The second scene takes place earlier at a Malibu beach house where a group of young men are watching a snuff movie.

> There's a young girl, nude, maybe fifteen, on a bed, her arms tied together above her head and her legs spread apart, each foot tied to a bedpost. She's lying on what looks like newspaper. . . . The camera cuts quickly to a young, thin, nude, scared-looking boy, sixteen, maybe seventeen, being pushed into the room by this fat black guy, who's also naked and who's got this huge hardon. . . . The black man ties the boy up on the floor, and I wonder why there's a chainsaw in the corner of the room, in the background, and then has sex with him and then he has sex with the girl and then walks off the screen. When he comes back he's carrying a box. It looks like a toolbox. . . . And he takes out an ice pick and what looks like a wire hanger and a package of nails and then a thin, large knife and he comes toward the girl and Daniel smiles and nudges me in the ribs. I leave quickly as the black man tries to push a nail into the girl's neck.

When the film is over, two of Clay's friends discuss what they have seen and speculate on whether or not it was a real portrayal of sexual mutilation and murder. And one of them says that since the owner of the film paid $15,000 for it, it has to be real. As Josephine Hendin has wisely observed, "The expensive snuff movie reveals a culture of acquisition carried to an extreme in the notion that death and mutilation are highs for sale," and "the superficial characterization employed . . . substitutes a rising body count for accumulated meaning."

And as the novel progresses, the body count continues to rise. In a third scene, which is virtually a real-life reenactment of the film, Clay goes to Rip's apartment and is taken into the bedroom where a twelve-year-old girl is lying on the mattress.

> Her legs are spread and tied to the bedposts and her arms are tied above her head. Her cunt is all rashed and looks dry and I can see that it's been shaved. She keeps moaning and murmuring words and moving her head from side to side, her eyes half-closed. Someone's put a lot of makeup on her, clumsily, and she keeps licking her lips, her tongue drags slowly, repeatedly, across them. Spin kneels by the bed and picks up a syringe and whispers something into her ear. The girl doesn't open her eyes. Spin digs the syringe into her arm. I just stare. Trent says "Wow."

In the next moments while the girl is sodomized and presumably raped by the various men present, Clay is moved to register his standard response, which is to feel vaguely ill, and he asks Rip, "Why?" Rip says, "If you want something, you have the right to take it. If you want to do something, you have the right to do it." And whether the thing you want to do is rape a young girl or snort some cocaine or eat at a fashionable restaurant or drive all night through the desert in your Mercedes convertible with the top down, it is all the same. It is all consumption; you have the right to do it; and it is all equally OK.

This philosophy of nihilistic consumership is operative throughout *Less Than Zero*, as it is in the two McInerney novels. But except in Rip's loutish declaration, it never assumes the form of a consciously held or enforced ideology.

It is simply taken for granted that all the characters in *Less Than Zero* will drive the most expensive cars, wear the most fashionable clothes, patronize the right restaurants and discos, and live in large mansions staffed by servants. These are the accepted material givens of the society being described, and since no monitory snobbery is required to maintain them (Who among Clay's friends would *not* consume the correct luxuries?), they are treated with a minimum of self-consciousness that is exactly commensurate with the minimum amount of consciousness the characters possess.

But this same philosophy, raised to the highest conceivable power of ugliness and rigorously enforced, becomes the central motivating influence behind Ellis's *American Psycho*, which has been the most widely discussed and heavily denounced novel in recent literary history. The ostensible cause of the controversy is the appallingly graphic depiction of acts of sexual mutilation and murder perpetrated mostly on women. And while that would appear to be reason enough for outrage, it seems to me that the real and even more disturbing cause lies deeper.

Ellis's narrator-protagonist is a young Wall Street financier named Patrick Bateman, and the first fact one learns about him is that he is passionately obsessive, even hysterically so, about correct sartorial and gastronomic procedures and is preoccupied with designer labels to the point where the greater part of the novel consists of a massive, pathologically meticulous listing of virtually every expensive product ever created by the high-fashion industry and the more modish purveyors of haute cuisine.

Passages like the following abound:

> The maître d' has sent over four complimentary Bellinis. . . . The Ronettes are singing "Then He Kissed

> Me," our waitress is a little hardbody and even Price seems relaxed though he hates the place. Plus there are four women at the table opposite ours, all great-looking—blond, big tits: one is wearing a chemise dress in double-faced wool by Calvin Klein, another is wearing a wool knit dress and jacket with silk faille bonding by Geoffrey Beene, another is wearing a symmetrical skirt of pleated tulle and an embroidered velvet bustier by, I think, Christian Lacroix plus high-heeled shoes by Sidonie Larizzi, and the last one is wearing a black strapless sequined gown under a wool crepe tailored jacket by Bill Blass. . . . We have to practically scream out our order to the hardbody waitress—who is wearing a bicolored suit of wool grain with passementerie trim by Myrone de Prémonville and velvet ankle boots and who . . . laughs sexily when I order, as an appetizer, the monkfish and squid ceviche with golden caviar; gives me a stare so steamy . . . when I order the gravlax pot pie with green tomatillo sauce. . . . Price orders the tapas and then the venison with yogurt sauce and fiddlehead ferns with mango slices. McDermott orders the sashimi with goat cheese and then the smoked duck with endive and maple syrup. Van Patten has the scallop sausage with the grilled salmon with raspberry vinegar and guacamole.

Early in the novel Bateman offers a lovingly narcissistic inventory of every last item of furnishings in his apartment, from which one, in order to maintain some, however fragile, hold on perspective, can safely provide only excerpts:

> Over the white marble and granite fireplace hangs an original David Onica. . . . The painting overlooks a long white down-filled sofa and a thirty-inch digital TV set from Toshiba, it's a high-contrast highly defined

> model plus it has a four-corner video stand with a high-tech tube combination from NEC with a picture-in-picture digital effects system (plus freeze-frame). . . . A hurricane halogen lamp is placed in each corner of the living room. Thin white venetian blinds cover all eight floor-to-ceiling windows. A glass-top coffee table with oak legs by Turchin sits in front of the sofa, with Steuben glass animals placed strategically around expensive crystal ashtrays from Fortunoff. . . . On the other side of the room, next to a desk and a magazine rack by Gio Ponti, is a complete stereo system . . . by Sansui with six-foot Duntech Sovereign 2001 speakers in Brazilian rosewood.

And on and on. We are then treated to a step-by-step description of exactly what Bateman does when he gets up in the morning. He wears Ralph Lauren silk pajamas and, after urinating, changes into Ralph Lauren monogrammed boxer shorts and a Fair Isle sweater and slides into silk polka-dot Enrico Hidolin slippers and stands in front of a chrome and acrylic Washmobile bathroom sink and pours Plax antiplaque formula into a stainless-steel tumbler and swishes it around his mouth for thirty seconds and then squeezes Rembrandt onto a faux-tortoiseshell toothbrush and starts brushing his teeth. This continues for several pages through breakfast, consisting of kiwi fruit, a sliced Japanese apple-pear (they cost four dollars each at Gristede's), oat-bran cereal with wheat germ and soy milk, and decaffinated herbal tea, and the ritual of getting dressed for the day in an Alan Flusser suit with soft-rolled peaked lapels, a dotted silk tie by Valentino Couture, and crocodile loafers by A. Testoni.

Bateman, in short, is clearly psychotic about procedural decorum in all its expensive, trendy, state-of-the-art manifestations. It is an obsession that provides him with constant reminders of who he is because it tells him that he is what he possesses, and it serves to shift his consciousness away from the vacuum that yawns beneath his peaked lapels.

This at least one infers about him from the first fifty or so pages of the novel. But then the atrocities begin and the truly unspeakable element begins to emerge. For while Bateman is passionately obsessed with decorum where style and taste are concerned, he is coldly dispassionate while committing the most heinous of crimes against the first principle of human decorum. That, it would seem, is the true obscenity of his story and the primary reason for the outrage it has provoked. But what is even worse, he commits his crimes in the name of the identical value system that governs the consumption of designer products. People in his view are things that have no identity—as he has none—beyond the kind of clothes they wear and the food they eat. Style, indeed, is the man and that is all he is. Therefore, people can be used, consumed, and discarded just as easily as any product. Their mutilation and murder constitute simply the ultimate high in a culture that is obsessed with the accumulation of material abundance but in which nothing consumed provides any real gratification—nothing, that is, short of mutilation and murder. Raised high enough on the bleak scale of depravity, this means that the taking of human life is no more important than buying an expensive designer suit. It is just more viscerally satisfying.

After killing one of his first victims, a homeless black man, Bateman describes himself as feeling "heady, ravenous, pumped up, as if I'd just worked out and endorphins are flooding my nervous system, or just embraced that first line of cocaine, inhaled the first puff of a fine cigar, sipped that first glass of Cristal." The sensation is excruciatingly intense, an almost orgasmic charge to the nerves and blood that no amount of designer consumership can possibly provide.

Yet this sort of response is rare, and the murders, as they multiply, become routine and mechanical and are finally no more or less exciting than the fashionable places and products that are interminably itemized. The same language is used to describe both killing and consuming, the precise details of mutilation and the precise cataloguing of labels, so that, compacted together, they become equated in value, and nothing results from them. In fact, nothing results from anything that happens in the novel because there is no coherently developing narrative. Bateman's evenings in restaurants and nightclubs, his workout sessions at the gym, his visits to videotape shops and his manicurist all take place any time or out of time. Each could occur anywhere in the novel, and the effect would be the same. Nothing, furthermore, results from Bateman himself, no contest or crisis of soul, no recognition of the evil he has done, no awareness of any good against which his actions might be measured and condemned. Not only is he indistinguishable from the stagnant, object-cluttered medium through which he moves, he is exactly as vapid and, therefore, finally as meaningless. He may arouse horror and indignation but not pity or understanding because no one ever learns what drives him, only that he is driven.

That is why he can tell us nothing new or vital about the nature of his derangement. As Norman Mailer said in his excellent *Vanity Fair* essay on the novel, "The failure of this book . . . is that by the end we know no more about Bateman's need to dismember others than we know about the inner workings in the mind of a wooden-faced actor who swings a broadax in an exploitation film." And that is what the novel finally becomes: a prose version of just such a film. It is no more enlightening about the criminal mind than *Nightmare on Elm Street*, and although it may be just as shocking, the shock lasts no longer and illuminates no deeper truth.

Yet in relation to the studies I have made up to now, there is this to be said about *American Psycho*: that even though it is far too bloated a novel to be classified as minimalist fiction, it can conceivably be read as the ultimate perverse statement of the minimalist vision of human experience. Ellis's narrative technique, for example, is an extreme exaggeration of the minimalist tendency to substitute lists of external environmental details for the creation of character from within, the result of which is that people in that fiction tend to take on no more meaning or value than the trivial surface features of the medium they inhabit. By the same token, Bateman is never created as a character but remains throughout a faceless embodiment of greed and compulsion to murder. Yet his environment of fashionable consumership is created in such minute detail that it becomes itself the only fully developed character in the novel.

But the most important resemblance the novel bears to minimalism consists of the fact that it carries to a logical conclusion, and far, far beyond, the view I earlier described as typical of so much minimalist fiction, the view "that human life in general and human experience in particular do not count for very much of anything and are equally consignable to oblivion." That is clearly the gruesome message of Ellis's novel.

■ CHAPTER VII ■

RIPENESS IS ALL

■

It is clearly a fault of nearly all the younger writers I have discussed that they have so little of substance to say about the nature of contemporary life—unless of course that fact tells us something about the nature of contemporary life, and I suspect it does. For we live in an age when reality tends more and more to present itself to our perceptions as sociology, when every problem, no matter how trivial or transient, is instantly brought up for examination and public debate, is measured and evaluated through statistical surveys of popular opinion or taken to court and made the subject of lawsuits. The result is that the problem is depersonalized and generalized into an abstract issue or case and is thereby removed from that private arena of personal loneliness, agony, humiliation, or remorse, where fiction in the past has always found its most vital materials.

When one thinks of the multitude of human difficulties that existed during those periods of history when no means were readily available for their solution, one begins to appreciate the advantages accruing to past writers of fiction. Consider, for instance, the enormous dramatic potential contained at one time in the terrible fate of pregnancy outside marriage—the public disgrace, the probable banishment of the unfortunate woman from family and community, perhaps even the ruin of her entire life because she has violated a double taboo: She has had sex before marriage, and she got pregnant from it. Dreiser's Clyde Griffiths in *An American Tragedy* involves his mistress, Roberta Alden, in just such a predicament, and, unspeakable cad that he is, he refuses to marry her because he is in love with the rich society girl, Sondra Finchley. To get Roberta out of the way, Clyde murders her and, as a consequence, is sentenced to die in the electric chair. Today Roberta could easily have had an abortion at any unpicketed Planned Parenthood clinic, while Clyde, with the help of a good lawyer, would probably have been acquitted on grounds of temporary insanity.

One wonders what would have happened if Thomas Wolfe's Eugene Gant had been young during the swinging sixties and been able to take easily to bed all those women, the sound of whose thighs rustling together in the berths of railroad Pullman cars used to drive him mad with lust. One thing that surely would have happened is that yards and yards of erotic dithyrambic prose would have been lost to literature forever.

Then there is the question of what might have transpired if Fitzgerald's Jay Gatsby had been persuaded, perhaps by the icily scornful Jordan Baker, that his vulgar display of wealth in an effort to impress Daisy Buchanan actually constituted a regressive reenactment of his childhood effort to please Mommy with an abundant display of the results of his bowel movement. And one can only ponder the effect on modern American fiction if someone with sufficient authority had convinced Hemingway that his heroes behaved with such macho toughness because he had grave secret doubts about his own masculinity and was very probably a repressed homosexual.

One could joke one's way through quite a long list of

instances. Among them: What would have happened to Raskolnikov if he had had access to psychiatric help, or to Emma Bovary if she could have had a divorce, or to Stephen Dedalus if he had been able to escape Ireland and get a Fulbright fellowship to travel to Norway and study his beloved Ibsen in the original. But the serious point is that none of these great stories would have been written, although the circumstances depicted in them would undoubtedly have been considerably more bearable.

Today there is a strong possibility that all these characters would be speedily drained of their individuality and dramatic value and turned into featureless statistical increments of some collective social dilemma. Emma would undoubtedly be swallowed up in the movement against the male oppression of women; Raskolnikov would be seen as a victim of a disadvantaged childhood; while Stephen would become an example of what happens to a person when he is differently abled, a poet among priests, in a society rife with religious authoritarian elitism.

A fair burlesque of this process can be witnessed almost any day on morning television. Eight or ten people are lined up before an audience. Today they are all battered wives; tomorrow they are all victims of child abuse; the next day they are all parents of children afflicted with birth defects; and the day after they are all men and women who, for the first time in their lives right there on the program, want to confess that they are gay or lesbian and just how miserable they have been, having to keep the secret from a homophobic society. All these people tell essentially the same unhappy story, but the audience is not seeing individual persons confessing before them. They are seeing interchangeable and anonymous manifestations of a variety of social problems, and it is the problems that are the stars of the program.

Perhaps the participants will gain some comfort from going public with their grief and describing it to the audience. It is also possible that there will be members of the audience who will gain some comfort from learning that others suffer from grief which they may have supposed they alone have experienced. But the public revelation displaces what was a private grief onto the collective and the impersonal, and private grief is a primary locus of drama for the writer.

It is of course the writer's traditional task to rescue the private grief from such abstracting and depersonalizing conditions and restore it to the context of the individual life by discovering the specific details through which the grief is manifested and that define it as unique to the situation and character of the person suffering from it.

But unfortunately, this is exactly the area in which the technique of minimalism adopted by so many of the younger writers has proved to be inadequate, for it does not permit the kind of large freedom necessary to document thoroughly enough the particular causes of a character's behavior or emotion. The minimalist writers are restricted by the very requirements of their chosen method to the surface appearances and fragmentary increments of experience and to the depiction largely of moments when something significant may or may not happen and they and their characters register their indifference or their bafflement in the face of what they do not understand. The quite trivial and pointless encounters portrayed in the stories of Amy Hempel and Frederick Barthelme are representative of the problem, and Boyle's retreat into the production of hermetically sealed fables that require no characterization in depth may indicate just how difficult the problem is to confront. In fact, the mood of malaise that permeates so much of the fiction I have discussed may well be the result not of some painfully achieved metaphysical despair but a depression subliminally felt by the writers themselves over their inability to treat their materials in such a way that they will fully signify and illuminate. It is also possible that they are depressed because, no matter what they do within their limited technical resources, the problems that afflict their characters are finally revealed to be indistinguishable from, and just as briefly diverting as, those aired on the talk shows. In other words, they are merely reflecting back in their fiction the official circumstances of distress that have become the sociological designer labels of our time: divorce, sexual incompatibility, substance abuse, crime, the traumas of gayness, the failure of communication between parents and child, the nullity of the overly affluent life.

Clearly, a major act of imagination would be required to repossess experience that has become the bankrupt property of cliché and infuse it with dramatic freshness and new meaning. And it happens that there are among the older generation of writers a number who have shown themselves capable of performing just such an act. In some of their novels Thomas Pynchon, William Gaddis, Norman Mailer, Joseph Heller, Kurt Vonnegut, and Don DeLillo have managed, not through minimalism but through a radical expansion of fiction into the areas of satire, fabulation, fantasy, and encyclopedic realism, to create entire fictional worlds composed of the concrete specifics of character and action that are treated with such originality that they escape ossification into clichés. I think of Pynchon's *Gravity's Rainbow*, Gaddis's *JR* and *The Recognitions,* Mailer's *Harlot's Ghost,* Heller's *Catch-22* and *Something Happened,* Vonnegut's *Slaughterhouse Five,* and DeLillo's *Players* and *White Noise.*

White Noise, in fact, is an excellent representative example of the kind of achievement I have described because in it DeLillo quite deliberately addresses the more ludicrous and clichéd features of contemporary life and through comic exaggeration inflates them into prime objects of satire. His narrator, a middle-aged academic named Jack Gladney, is chairman of the department of Hitler studies at the College-on-the-Hill and teaches a seminar in Advanced Nazism. His wife, Babette, teaches a course in sitting, standing, and walking. His best friend, Murray Jay Siskind, is a member of the Popular Culture Department, a lecturer on living icons, an authority on Elvis Presley, and teaches a course in the cinema of car crashes. These characters exist in an environment that is vibrant with the nearly subliminal hum and buzz of high-tech electronic devices designed to ease the labors of life and promote health and happiness. Yet it soon becomes evident that the environment is the villainous central character of the novel, and the people are its prisoners and victims.

They live in constant anxiety over the state of their health, and since their days are trivialized, they lie awake at night and worry about when they are going to die. Everywhere the landscape swarms with joggers running from death and the void they sense but cannot confront within themselves. In trying to curb her desire to smoke, Babette worries over whether to chew sugared or sugarless gum. The sugared will add to her weight problem, but the sugarless has been shown to cause cancer in laboratory rats. The local grade school has to be evacuated because there may be chemical contamination or something carcinogenic in the ventilating system. The children "were getting headaches and eye irritations. . . . A teacher rolled on the floor and spoke foreign languages." The Gladney family limits their television watching ("Television is just another name for junk mail") to one night a week. "The effect would be to de-glamorize the medium" in the eyes of the children, "make it wholesome domestic sport. Its narcotic undertow and eerie diseased brain-sucking power would be gradually reduced." The Gladney's brilliant young son plays chess by mail with a convicted killer serving a life sentence and is so obsessed with the principles of relativity and parallax that he cannot say for certain that it is raining outside even as he and his father are at that moment driving through the rain. It is all very like the kitsch and dreck world portrayed by Donald Barthelme in his shorter fiction. But where DeLillo is concerned, one feels that there is an alert and highly disciplined mind at work behind the portrait.

In some of his earlier novels the characters are attracted to terrorism or international espionage because the drama has drained out of most of the experiences that once gave them some assurance that they were alive. Having vicariously experienced everything through the media, they yearn to become involved in events that can be intensely and personally felt. Afloat as they are in a soupy sea of technological trivia, enclosed as they are in a plastic bubble of narcissism, they crave to be brought violently to life by direct contact with violence.

In DeLillo's fifth novel, *Players*, for example, the young couple, Lyle and Pammy Wynant, are totally abstracted from the places of their work and can find no meaning in their functions—he trading on the Stock Exchange, she writing promotional literature for a firm called Grief Management Council, a personal-services organization that sells information on how to control one's emotions so that the pain of grief will scarcely be felt at all.

Two occurrences out in the real world dislodge the Wynants from their catatonia, one initiated by violence, the other resulting in violence, and both are attractive to them because they promise to open a way to feeling and adventure and offer at least temporary escape from an existence completely without point.

In *White Noise* the Gladney family watch disaster occurring elsewhere and always to other people out there in the vast nullity of the television screen. "We were . . . watching houses slide into the ocean, whole villages crackle and ignite in a mass of advancing lava. Every disaster made us wish for more, for something bigger, grander, more sweeping." They want, above all, to be awakened from the abstraction of vicarious media experience and forced to confront reality rather than its distant image. And reality obliges by bringing disaster to them in the form of a poisonous black cloud that arises from a wrecked tank car and threatens to asphyxiate the townspeople.

As the Gladneys join the stream of traffic fleeing the cloud, they are brought momentarily to life, stirred to an awareness that for the first time they are fighting against their environment for survival instead of being anesthetized by it. It is, therefore, not surprising that the brilliant, overly analytical son should react to the experience with a kind of excitement he has never before displayed.

"He spoke enthusiastically," says his father, "with a sense of appreciation for the vivid and unexpected. . . . It hadn't occurred to me that one of us might find these events brilliantly stimulating. He talked about the snow, the traffic, the trudging people. He speculated on how far we were from the abandoned camp. . . . I'd never heard him go on about something with such spirited enjoyment. . . . Was this some kind of end-of-the-world elation? Did he seek distraction from his own small miseries in some violent and overwhelming event? His voice betrayed a craving for terrible things."

And terrible things do ultimately happen to both Jack and Babette Gladney. But the virtue of the novel consists of DeLillo's extraordinary insights into some of the darker truths of the way we live now, truths that in his satiric treatment of them are dislodged from the deadening encrustations of cliché surrounding them and given fresh dramatic meaning.

DeLillo, Pynchon, Gaddis, Mailer, and the others have brought to the production of what is clearly major fiction intellectual and imaginative strengths that their younger contemporaries (with the exception of Moore and Boyle) show very few signs of possessing. One cannot help wondering, therefore, on the basis of what resources they will be able to continue their careers and expand and deepen their talents. They appear on the whole to have only moderate intellectual culture. They evidently possess very little critical or satirical perspective on contemporary life, slight knowledge of the past, and apparently no sense that they belong to a literary tradition that might prove nourishing if they were able and willing to learn from it. In fact, one might argue that judging by the evidence of their work, they have no particular interest even in literature and possess nothing like the vast literary erudition of Gaddis, Pynchon, and Mailer.

The problem they face is one that the schools of creative writing have not addressed and cannot. Those schools have provided many of them with a certain technical facility in the writing of prose, and some of them have been taught sufficiently well to become truly accomplished stylists. But style alone will take them just so far, and in this advanced phase of our literary sophistication, that is not nearly far enough.

▪ INDEX ▪

ACJ5389 7/28/92

PS
379
A5198
1992